The Widow's Hour

L L MOMON

To be trusted is a greater compliment than being loved.

George MacDonald

To the readers

The Widow's Hour is a cross between a romantic suspense and psychological thriller novel. It isn't urban fiction, but an emotionally charged slow burn. This story follows a woman navigating death, grief, quiet threats, and the possibility of love—all at the same time.

Thank you for trusting me with your time, your emotions, and this journey. I hope *The Widow's Hour* keeps you turning pages late into the night and leaves you satisfied come morning.

L.L. Momon

Read This

Everyone isn't for you and everyone doesn't want you to win. Remember, the enemy's job is to kill, steal and destroy. We have to be diligent in vetting the people we let around us. The bible says guard your heart above all else for everything you do flows from it. Surround yourself with people that carry good hearts but don't forget to protect yours in the process. With that being said...Test every spirit you encounter and I do mean every spirit. Not just test it though but ask our Heavenly Father for discernment on how to deal with such spirit.

I love y'all and there is absolutely nothing you can do about it.

Chapter One

I kicked off my heels the moment I stepped inside my Buckhead mansion, the echo bounced off white marble floors and ceilings that suddenly felt too big, too cold, and empty for a house that had just buried a man with an eight-figure net worth and a reputation built on polished lies.

Atlanta's elite had shown out earlier, designer black dresses, diamonds glistening in the sun, luxury cars lined down the street like it was a damn fashion show instead of a funeral. But not one of them looked at me with sympathy. They never believed I deserved him, and now they damn sure didn't believe I wasn't the reason he was gone. I didn't give a shit what they thought. It was fuck those people as far as I was concerned.

Slipping out of my black, fitted, elegant funeral dress, I

let the fabric fall like a potato sack at my feet. It still carried the faint scent of roses from the funeral spray. Everyone had cried today, not for my husband, but for the money, the parties, the image. Glancing over at the mirror that stretched from floor to ceiling, I almost didn't recognize the woman staring back at me. She looked worn and tired.

My curls, which had been pinned into a sleek low bun for the service, were already trying to push free. After a long, arduous day, it felt phenomenal getting out of my clothes and letting my hair down. I had grown tired of being pristine and polished, especially for people who didn't give a damn about me and only wanted to see me break. Those bitches would choke on their insecurities first, because I would never let them witness that.

I walked into my husband's office, a room I was never welcomed in. He always said it was for business, but the real reason was control, power, and secrets he put extra effort into hiding. Plopping down in his expensive leather chair, I thought about the days leading up to his death.

After a bomb evening of hanging with my girls, cackling and talking shit, dancing, smoking hookah, and drinking countless White Russians, I sashayed out of the restaurant looking and feeling good, without a care in the world. I called Jahi several times before leaving the bar to let him know I had something for him once I got home, but my calls went unanswered. I never bothered leaving voicemails. What was the use? He wouldn't have checked them anyway.

I could feel eyes on me before I even stepped off the curb. The Atlanta night was buzzing. Traffic hummed down Peachtree, while neon lights bounced off glass buildings. The air was thick with expensive perfume and hot wings. But something about that night felt off and unsettling, like God was tapping me on the shoulder, telling me to be careful.

Tightening the belt on my cream trench coat, I crossed the valet lane of the Buckhead Ritz. I lingered under the soft glow of the entrance lights, letting my eyes adjust to the night. Buckhead looked normal, valet boys laughing, couples waiting on their rideshares, rich men and their sugar babies creeping on the low. But underneath it all, I felt something or someone watching me. Something I couldn't quite put my finger on yet.

My phone buzzed.

> Unknown Number: Where are you bouncing off to?

I froze. Not again. This was the second message this week. Same tone, same audacity. Never an introduction or a clue of who it was, just direct access to my life like they had a front-row seat. It pissed me off to no end.

Inhaling slowly, I pushed down the knot rising in my

throat and scanned the parking lot with a little more intention. That's when I noticed it.

A black sedan parked midway down the ramp, engine still running. Tint dark enough to hide secrets.

Stepping off the curb, I made my way toward my Benz. Heels clicking slowly but steady. I didn't want to look like I was running, even though my instincts were screaming that I should have been. When I unlocked the door, my phone vibrated again. I stood still.

> Unknown Number: Tell him you're loyal. He doesn't believe you are.

Him?

I didn't need context. There was only one him in my life. He had to be responsible for these random messages, but what I couldn't understand was why he wasn't sending them himself.

Jahi.

My husband, or at least the version of him the world still believed in.

He was Atlanta's golden boy. Educated, polished, structured, ambitious. Handsome Black excellence wrapped in tailored suits and a smile that fooled investors, church mothers, pastors, and half the city council. People loved him.

But somewhere between the charity galas and board

meetings, between power-couple photos and the pressure to be perfect, something shifted. He got colder. I got quieter. And suspicion filled the space where love used to be.

I wasn't cheating or stepping out, nor did I possess the energy to sneak around in shadows with anyone else. I was simply exhausted from pretending we were still the couple everyone bragged about. And lately, it felt like Jahi was looking for someone else to blame for the cracks he was causing.

Sliding into the driver's seat, I closed the door, and exhaled. My heartbeat was loud, too present. I started the engine and turned the stereo up, hoping sound and movement would shake the tension loose. But when I checked the mirror, the sedan pulled out too. Smooth and silent with no hesitation.

My anxiety spiked.

He doesn't believe you're loyal replayed in my head like a broken record.

I couldn't believe he actually had someone following me, like I was the one staying out all night, getting random phone calls in the early morning, or coming home in the middle of the night. That's what he did, not me.

Turning down Peachtree, I kept my speed steady. My eyes flicked between the road and the rearview mirror. The sedan kept perfect pace, never passing, never falling back.

My stomach dropped.

I seriously couldn't believe he didn't trust me. Especially to the point that he had someone following me. This pissed me off because I had never given him a reason to doubt me. I'd shown him loyalty and respect even when I shouldn't have. His ass didn't deserve it, but I did because he was my husband. This had to be about something else.

Maybe it was fear. His fear of exposure. Of secrets slipping. Of me becoming a liability in a life he'd curated too carefully. He sure as hell didn't have to worry about that. Because if his life blew up, mine would too, and I wasn't going for that shit.

I turned onto a side street near Phipps, one I used all the time. The sedan followed, closer now, riding my bumper. My grip tightened the steering wheel until my fingers went numb.

Just as I hit the light, another message came through.

> Unknown Number: He's not the only one watching you. Be careful. Watch your back.

With that message, everything inside me quaked.

Whatever I thought I understood went out the window. This was bigger than Jahi's insecurity. Bigger than our failing marriage and bigger than someone checking up on me.

This was the moment my life shifted, with no warning, no explanation, and no turning back.

I finally made it home, safe and unscathed. Reaching my gate, I waited patiently for it to open. It felt like it took ages, though only twenty seconds passed. Driving up the horseshoe driveway, I checked behind me for the thousandth time before raising the garage door and exiting my car.

My nerves were rattled because I didn't know who was behind that wheel of that car or who was sending those text messages. But more than anything, I was pissed at the audacity of my husband.

I shook it off as I entered my house. It was the newest and fanciest on the block, but that was all it was to me. It wasn't a home. There was nothing inviting or cozy about it. Just a beautiful shell. One void of all the things that made a house feel like a home. Feelings, love, care and tenderness didn't live here anymore.

I went upstairs to confront Jahi about having someone trail me, only to find him sprawled across the bed naked, a towel draped loosely over his center. Once I saw that bulge, confrontation could wait. His dick was calling my name.

I disrobed, flipped the towel back, and took his soft flesh into my mouth, sucking gently until I felt his pulse thump against my tongue.

"Damn, baby," he groaned. "It's been a while since you

woke me up like this. That feels so fucking good. I take it you had a good time with your girls tonight."

I nodded yes, mouth full of dick as his hands trickled up my body for something to please. He started with my nipples, twisting them gently until they pebbled like rocks.

"Wait, Nuri. Let me get in on this," he moaned. "I wanna taste you too." That was music to my ears because sex between us had been few and far between. His eagerness gave me a little glimmer of hope by participating in my horniness.

I flipped around, hovering my pussy over his lips while still pleasuring him. His tongue found my center, and he lapped at my clit. Sucking and licking while I rocked my hips. It felt so damn good. We continued enjoying one another until I creamed down his chin.

Jahi had major stamina, so I knew his nut wouldn't come as easy. He often made me work very hard for it. Tonight didn't seem any different. After I climaxed, I hopped on all fours, arching my back as deep as I could.

"I love when you come home and put that wet wet on me. You look so fucking sexy, and I know you want this dick. I can already feel that pussy thumping," he groaned as he entered me from the back.

I purred with delight as I felt the pressure in my yoni. "You feel lucky, huh? Well show me. Stroke this pussy and make me cum again."

And stroke me he did. He fucked me like he really loved me or really hated me. It was hard to tell these days. But tonight, every time he felt his love rising, he would drop down and eat my pussy again. He was stalling me out, and he knew this drove me crazy. I was the edging queen, and he was the teasing king. We were a match made in heaven when it came to pleasing each other. He flipped me over and kissed me like he was starving. Not gentle or careful, but rough and passionate. Almost animalistic. My fingers threaded through his hair as he slid into me once again.

I hated how he knew exactly what my body needed. Moving in sync, his mouth traced my neck...then my collarbone. All the places he knew drove me crazy, and I let it happen because I had no idea when it would happen again. In moments like this, he felt like mine again. Fully attentive and present. I wanted to stay like this forever. In that space where his forehead rested against mine, where our breathing and heartbeats synced, where I could pretend this was what our love still looked like every day.

I wanted to feel wanted, and for that brief time, I did. I wanted this to be our reset. I wanted to believe that sex as good as this would be the answer to all our problems. That unbelievable orgasms could fix everything, but as soon as his body stiffened at the end... I felt the disconnect immediately. I knew him too well.

He pulled back just slightly after, his eyes softening then drifting. He kissed my forehead instead of my lips, and that was always the sign. I stayed curled against him longer than I should have. Pretending not to notice the emotional distance settling back in. The warmth between us was already cooling.

Eventually, I rolled over to my side of the bed and stared at the ceiling while he got up and headed to the bathroom. He coldly threw me a rag and closed the bathroom door.

"Babe, I'm going to head down to my office for a few. There are some things I need to catch up on. I'd like not to be disturbed."

I didn't even look up, and there was no use in arguing. He wouldn't have listened anyway.

My voice cracked, "Ok, babe. I'm going to sleep."

Pissed at the thought, and angry at my husband, I drifted off to sleep.

The next morning felt wrong from the moment I opened my eyes. The house was too quiet. Too still and just felt heavy. Even with the sun pouring through the sheer curtains, I felt a layer of dread clinging to my skin... whatever whispered to me last night in the car hadn't finished speaking. I didn't even get the chance to ask Jahi about that black sedan before he hauled ass away from me.

Slowly moving through my bedroom, I glanced at the

emptiness on his side of the bed. I tied my robe before pushing my curls into a messy bun. My phone was faced down on the nightstand, and I hadn't checked it since I made it home. And I didn't want to. I wasn't ready to see if another message came through. I also wasn't ready to admit that my marriage had drifted into a place I no longer recognized. Pushing my thoughts to the side, I walked to the kitchen, letting the marble floors cool my feet, and started a pot of coffee. I needed caffeine to help clear the fog in my head. That's when the doorbell rang.

My heart stuttered. Nobody ever rang my doorbell, not without texting first. The gate sensors usually sent an alert to my phone regarding anyone approaching, so the silence made me uneasy. I checked the screen on my phone for any alerts I may have missed, then I checked the gate cameras. They were open wide, and this left me confused. I could have sworn they closed behind me as I sped up my driveway. I checked the time. It was 8:17 a.m. I swallowed hard and walked to the foyer to peek through the side window.

A man stood at my door. Mid 40s maybe, with a salt and pepper beard. He wore a dark suit that didn't quite fit like a tailored suit, but it was nice enough. His hands were tucked into his jacket pockets, and he kept glancing up and down the street like he didn't trust the open air. When I cracked the door, he didn't smile.

"Mrs. Nuri Laurent?"

My chest tightened. "Yes?"

"My name is Reid Mercer. I'm a private investigator. I need to speak with you. It's urgent and about your husband."

The world went still. I opened the door wider, but not by much. "What about Jahi?"

He shifted, almost uncomfortable. "May I please come in?"

"No," my voice came out steady, but my skin prickled with heat. "I don't know you, so say what you need to say right here. I've had some pretty creepy shit happening to me lately, and I'm not really trusting anybody right now."

He nodded slowly, as if he expected that.

"Mrs. Laurent... Jahi hired me six months ago. To follow you."

I didn't respond. I just stared.

"He thought you may have been involved with someone else," the investigator continued. "But in the end, that wasn't all he ended up needing me for."

"Well don't just stand there looking crazy. Talk," I snapped. "That's why you're here, isn't it? What else did he need from you? What was the job?"

"To make sure you were safe. That's initially what he told me. But after a while... it started feeling like he was hiding you from someone or something." He paused. "Or hiding someone from you. I honestly don't know what was happening, but I just know something was off. You needed to know."

"Wait, does he know you're here? He's down in his office. He asked not to be disturbed, but I don't think he'd mind because what in the fuck are you talking about?"

"Mrs. Laurent. He isn't in his office. I can assure you of that."

"Oh yeah, well tell me, Mr. Private Investigator. How the fuck do you know?"

His expression changed into something softer. Like regret or sympathy.

"I know because...Mrs. Laurent— Jahi died last night."

Chapter Two

The air left my lungs so fast I had to steady myself on the doorframe.

"Wait, what? What do you mean died?" I whispered, barely audible.

"He had an accident on I-285 around two this morning. It was terrible. His car caught fire. The first responders couldn't... they couldn't get to him in time. I'm so sorry."

I took a step back, shaking my head. "No. No, this has got to be some kind of mistake. This isn't real. There is no way you... you are telling me that my husband is gone. He said he was going to his office. He didn't say anything about leaving the house. This can't be real. It can't."

Mercer didn't move forward. He stayed rooted on the porch with the calm of a man who'd delivered this kind of news before.

"I'm terribly sorry," he said quietly.

My ears rang. I felt like the world was tilting. Just last night... just hours ago... I was convincing myself that I didn't recognize my husband anymore. That I didn't love or need him. Now he was gone. Just like that. I swallowed hard, but my voice still came out broken.

"Why are you here? Why did you come tell me this instead of the police?"

"Because your husband left something for you." Mercer reached inside his jacket slowly, like he was handling something fragile. "A letter. He mailed it to my office a couple days ago with instructions to deliver it to you only if something happened to him."

I stared at the cream-colored envelope he extended. My name was written in Jahi's handwriting. My hands trembled as he placed it in my palms.

Reid Mercer cleared his throat. "Mrs. Laurent... your husband was scared. I don't know who he crossed, and he never told me. But he kept saying someone was watching him. That he didn't know how to fix what was fucked up."

My head began to throb, and my vision started to blur. My chest felt too tight for my ribs. I whispered, "Someone was watching me too, and they followed me last night."

Reid nodded once. "I know. I'm the one that sent you those text messages. I followed the car that was following you. I lost them after they turned off East Wild Horse Road. That wasn't one of my people."

My head began to swoon, and my knees grew weak.

"Why would anyone be watching me or following me for that matter? I haven't done shit. Hell, I'm about as straight-laced as they come."

His eyes turned shifty, like he was holding back something heavy. "I don't know," he said. "I truly don't. The answer to that question may have died with your husband... or you may be holding the answer in your hands. You will never know until you open that letter."

My fingers clutched the envelope. This letter could hold the truth, lies, a confession, or help me make sense of our life for the past few years.

Before Reid stepped off the porch, he turned back.

"One more thing, Mrs. Laurent. Your husband wasn't suspicious of you because he thought you were cheating. He was suspicious because he thought someone might have been using you to get to him."

For a long moment after he left, I stood there, robe loosely tied, with the letter trembling in my hand. The morning light was suddenly too harsh against my eyes. I left the gate open because I knew once the news got out about Jahi... it would only be a matter of time before my house would become a circus.

The news didn't feel real. Neither did this world I was

living in. It felt detached... staged. Something inside my body had broken, and my brain was still trying to catch up to the pain. I was trying to make sense of it. Closing the door slowly, I leaned back against it, letting myself slide until I was sitting on the cold marble floor. My fingers wrapped around the letter like it was the last thing anchoring me to reality.

Jahi. Dead. My husband. The man I spent nearly a decade trying to understand. Gone in the middle of the night. Why did he leave this fucking house? Who was he going to meet? My chest tightened until breathing felt like a chore. Grief didn't just sneak up on me or hit me gently. It smacked me like a ton of bricks and cracked open old memories like a Brazilian nut. I'd complained about him leaving me alone all the time. Now I was alone permanently, and it stung like a thousand hornets to my heart.

I wiped my face with shaking hands. Why does it hurt like this when we weren't even okay? We were not in a good place at all. I hated myself for asking that question, but it sat heavy on my shoulders. The truth was complicated and painful. I loved him once... loudly, publicly, and with the kind of devotion people envied.

Jahi and I met at a charity gala for the Get Em Boys Youth Foundation. I remembered the shimmer of the crystal lights, the laughter of Atlanta's elite, and the clinking of champagne glasses... and then Jahi walking toward me with that calculated, charismatic, magnetic confidence. I had been drawn to it. To him. To the stability he promised. To the partnership he painted like a future we could build together, and we did.

He was the man my parents loved. The one my family's boardroom smiled at. The one the *Atlanta Journal* photographed next to me at every event. I thought he was a safe choice, but now I wasn't sure. I wasn't sure about anything but the fact that I was losing it. I closed my eyes and whispered to God, "Why?"

The memories weren't all bad. Our earlier years held soft, intimate kisses at midnight. Trips to the Maldives in the middle of the week. Flowers, gifts and even properties just because. We shared our dreams and ambitions, and endless nights overlooking the city from penthouse balconies. But then came the coldness and the secrets. The distance I could never quite explain to anyone. Not even myself. It was like one day he loved me fiercely and the next he didn't.

Jahi knew the relationship I'd had with my parents and the way it affected me in adulthood. It caused major abandonment issues. He struggled to understand how I experienced abandonment while growing up in a two-parent household. The concept was so foreign to him.

I had to explain time and time again... while I was under my parents' roof, they weren't. They were busy building an empire, which left me to see about myself half the time. The other half was spent defending my every action against my mother. Because of my history, I was needy, clingy, and very insecure. He promised me he could love me through it all, and for a while, it seemed like he tried.

My neediness didn't go away because he became the big man around town. If anything, it was heightened. I always felt something would eventually pull him away from me. I'd never imagined in my wildest dreams it would be death at forty-two.

A knock pulled me from my reverie. This knock was firmer. Urgent.

I stood up on legs that didn't feel like mine and opened the door. Two uniformed officers stood on my porch. One older Black woman with soft, warm eyes and a younger man standing slightly behind her.

"Mrs. Laurent?" the woman asked.

I nodded.

"I'm Sergeant Lawson. This is Officer Kennedy. May we come in?"

I didn't trust my voice, so I simply stepped aside. They moved into the foyer with quiet respect, glancing at my disheveled robe.

"I'm very sorry, ma'am," Sergeant Lawson began softly. "We're here to notify you of your husband's passing. There was an accident on I-285 early this morning. He—"

"He's dead. I already know," I said somberly, cutting her off mid-sentence. "I... I was told just a little while ago. I'm still trying to process and truly grasp what is happening around me. This shit doesn't feel real."

The sergeant nodded gently. "Yes, I understand. But how did you know? We hadn't released your husband's name, so no one should be aware," she said, looking befuddled.

I opened my mouth to tell her about Mr. Mercer but decided against it.

"Umm, a friend of mine called. She was out this morning and just so happened to ride by the accident. She recognized his car. After all... it was the only one like it in this city. Sergeant Lawson... this is Atlanta. Everybody is always minding someone else's business," I muttered quickly.

"Well, it is protocol and a matter of respect that we show up and deliver the news to the family. Speaking of family... are you alone in this house?"

"I am. Why do you ask?"

Sergeant Lawson hesitated. "Because you shouldn't be alone at a time like this. Also, Mrs. Laurent... there are some details we'll need to go over later. But right now... do you have someone you can call?"

My eyes began to water. That word, *alone*, hit me heavy. I felt it everywhere.

"Yes… I'll call my girls," I whispered.

The officers offered condolences again, gave me their cards, told me I would receive a call to go to the county coroner to identify the body if possible, and stepped out as quietly as they entered. As soon as the door closed, my fingers shook as I dialed the first number I could think of.

Charity

Witty. Brilliant. Always two steps ahead. She gave Jahi a business card at one of the charity galas, and I found it in his wallet. I called her to come at her as a woman, and she cursed me out. We laughed about it and became fast friends after I realized she wanted my man's business… not my man. She was a PR powerhouse and my "make it make sense" friend. She picked up on the first ring.

"Ummm, Mrs. Ma'am, why are you calling me at—"

"Hello?" I mumbled.

Her tone shifted instantly. "Nuri? Baby, what's wrong with your voice?"

"He's gone," I choked. "Jahi… he died in a car crash this morning."

There was a long, stunned silence before I heard the sound of a purse zipping and keys jangling.

"I'm on the way. Don't move. Don't breathe wrong. I'm coming."

Paige

Sassy, with a wild tongue and unmatched comedic timing. Linked up in middle school and had been friends ever since. She was the friend who would bring food, shade, and violence in that order. She played no games and didn't have an ounce of tact.

"Paige—"

"Nuri Surai Laurent, why are you crying like that? What his ass do or didn't do now?"

Another pause.

"He's dead," I blurted out.

Paige didn't respond for a full ten seconds. Then—

"I'm coming. I'm grabbing my shoes and a hoodie. If you need me to fight death itself, just tell me where his ass is at."

Maya

Quiet. Sweet with church-girl energy. I met her in a Facebook group years back when I was searching for a new church home. She DMed me with an invite, and we were locked in from that moment. She was the mother of the group even though she didn't have kids yet. Her voice came in soft and warm.

"Hey, honey, what's—"

"Maya..."

"He's gone. My husband is gone. He passed in a car accident around two this morning."

"Oh, Nuri." Her voice trembled. "I'm praying as I grab my keys. I'll be there in fifteen minutes."

When I hung up, I sank onto the staircase, pressing the unopened letter to my chest. Three friends were racing to be by my side. The private investigator had dropped a truth bomb that shook me to my core, and the police had confirmed the worst. None of this made sense to me. Not yet, anyway.

Beneath my grief, beneath my shock, beneath the ache of losing a man I wasn't sure I still loved... something else stirred.

Fear.

Because whatever was in this letter... my husband only wanted me aware if he didn't make it out alive.

And that could have meant his death wasn't just an accident.

Chapter Three

Before the ladies arrived, I sat at the edge of the couch with my phone in my hand for a long time before I pressed the call button. I kept staring at Jahi's name in my contacts like it might blink back to life and tell me all this shit wasn't real.

The phone rang once, twice, and my breath caught when his mother answered. Her voice was warm and unsuspecting.

"Hi, Mama." My throat went dry immediately. "It's Nuri."

"Oh, hey baby!" she said brightly. "I was just about to call you. Where is my Jahi? I didn't receive my morning call like I usually do."

My chest caved in.

"I—" I swallowed hard, and my voice trembled. "I'm sorry. He... he won't be calling today or any other day."

There was a pause. No alarm yet. Just confusion.

"What do you mean, Nuri?" his father asked in the background. I could hear the chair scrape as he stood up. "Mama, put me on speaker, please."

She did. I heard the faint echo shift.

"Nuri?" his father said firmly. "What's going on?"

I closed my eyes. "Jahi passed away early this morning. It happened around two a.m."

The phone went silent. There was no crying or yelling. Just bone-chilling silence.

"That's not funny," his mother finally said, her voice suddenly small. "Why would you joke like that?"

"I wouldn't. I swear I would never joke about something like that."

His father cleared his throat. "Say it again, baby girl."

"Jahi is gone. The police came this morning and told me. They just left. It was a car accident."

His mother let out a sharp, broken sound I'd never heard before. It made my blood run cold.

"No... no, no. That can't be right. I just talked to him yesterday. He said he'd see us this weekend." Her voice cracked. "He promised."

I pressed my palm to my mouth, tears spilling freely now. "I know he did."

His father spoke again, but his voice had changed. It was now lower, unsteady. "Where is he?"

"They took him to the county," I said softly. "I haven't seen him yet, and they may not let me. The car caught fire, and I'm not exactly sure if they are going to let me view him."

His mother cried openly now, grief pouring through the phone like a flood.

"That's my baby," she wailed. "That's my son. God, not my child..."

I felt useless. Helpless. Like no words could reach them.

"I'm so sorry," I said over and over. "I'm so sorry."

There was another stretch of silence. It was thick and unbearable.

"We're coming," his father said at last. "We're coming to Atlanta as soon as we can get a flight out. Just give us some time, baby girl. We will be there."

"Okay," I nodded, even though they couldn't see me. "I'll be here," I whispered.

His mother sniffed hard. "Nuri..."

The line went quiet again before she added, barely audible, "Please go be with him. Please don't let him be alone."

"I won't," I promised. "As soon as they let me. I'll be there."

When the call ended, I sat there holding my phone like it might ring again and tell me I dreamed the whole thing, but it didn't. After the phone call and hearing his mother's screams, the truth finally settled in my bones. My husband was really gone.

The phone call to his parents snatched every ounce of strength I had in my body. I was emotionally exhausted, but I still had to call my parents to let them know their golden boy was gone. I didn't want them to hear it from anyone else. I stared at my phone longer than I should have because I had to prepare myself for my mother and her dramatics.

Calling Jahi's parents had nearly broken me, but calling my parents was different. Worse. It felt dangerous.

Because my mother didn't grieve quietly. She performed it, and I knew before I even heard her voice, she would say something to piss me off. She always did.

Drawing in a sharp breath, I finally pressed the button.

"Hello?" Her voice was sharp, impatient. "Nuri? We're going to have to talk later. I'm about to step into a call."

"Mom," I said quickly. "Please don't hang up."

"What is it now, Nuri?"

I swallowed long and hard before I spoke again. "It's Jahi."

Once again, silence.

"What about him? Is he late again? Because if he missed that meeting with—"

"Mom," I interrupted, my voice shaking. "Jahi passed away. He's dead."

The pause was brief. Then—

"What?" she shrieked. "What do you mean passed away?"

"He died last night. There was an accident."

"Oh my God," she gasped loudly, too loudly. "Jesus Christ, Nuri! What kind of accident? Where was he? Why wasn't he with you?"

Each question came faster than the last, like bullets.

"I don't know everything yet. The police came this morning. Right now, they're investigating."

She sucked in a breath so sharp it sounded theatrical. "Oh, this is not happening. This is absolutely not happening."

I closed my eyes.

"Your father just stepped out for a meeting," she continued. "Do you have any idea how this will affect this company when this gets out? Jahi worked with us. People respected and relied on him. What in the fuck are we to do now?"

I flinched. *People respected him. Relied on him. Not you loved him. Not are you okay.*

"Is that all you have to say, Mother? I thought you'd

want to know and needed to hear it from me," I said quietly.

"What do you want me to say? Of course I needed to know," she snapped. "But why didn't you call sooner? What were you doing? Sitting around?"

I felt heat rise up my neck. "I just found out this morning."

She gasped again, louder than before. "So you just... waited? Nuri, do you hear yourself?"

I clenched my jaw. "Mom..."

"Was he with you last night?"

The question landed heavy.

"Yes and no. We were together, but then he left," I said. "We—"

"Oh," she cut in. "So you two were fighting again."

"That's not—"

"I warned you," she continued. "I told you your attitude was pushing that man away. A woman doesn't get distant with her husband and expect everything to stay intact."

Sucking in a deep breath, I muttered, "Please don't do this."

"I'm just being honest," she said coldly. "Stress does things. Neglect does things. Men don't just get up and leave their houses for no reason in the middle of the night.

You must have done something to make him leave. What did you say? Did you piss him off?"

I stood up, my hands shaking now. "Are you really sitting here on this fucking phone blaming me?"

"Watch your language, you little twit. I'm simply saying," she replied carefully, "that if you had been more present, more supportive, maybe he wouldn't have been wherever he was."

I snapped. "I did not kill my husband, and I couldn't control his every fucking move. Jahi did what he wanted, when he wanted, so none of this is my fucking fault." My voice trembled with fury.

She scoffed. "No one said that. But perception matters, Nuri. And right now, this doesn't look good."

I stared at the wall, stunned. "Mom, my husband is gone. Do you really think I give a fuck about what people will think? Or what this looks like? Fuck those people. My life is about to change, and I don't know what that means for me, and all you can think about is what people will say or think. You are fucking unbelievable."

"I'm sorry if what I'm saying hurts your feelings. But you should indeed care what people say. Trust me, people will talk. Look at the situation. A young, beautiful woman, marriage problems, sudden death—"

"That's enough," I said sharply.

She kept going. "And now we're going to have to

manage this. The board will ask questions. The church will ask questions. Do you know how stressful this will be for us, for the company?"

Tears stung my eyes, not from grief, but rage. "I didn't call you for this. I called because my husband is dead, and I thought that maybe, just maybe, you'd have something useful to say. I should have fucking known better."

"Well, maybe if you had been a better wife—"

Click.

I didn't say goodbye, nor did I wait for her to finish. I just ended the call because my mother had officially lost her damn mind. Before I said something that I couldn't take back, I hung up. She is and has always been a miserable fucking soul.

I stood there with the phone still pressed to my ear, my chest heaving and my hands numb. That was the moment I knew I was truly alone in this, and whatever came next... whatever Jahi left behind... I was going to face it without my parents' approval, protection, or permission.

Grief was one thing, but being blamed for it?

That was unforgivable.

Fuck her.

Chapter Four

By the time I heard tires crunching down my driveway, I'd changed into leggings and a soft crewneck I stole from Jahi years ago. It smelled faintly like him—Bvlgari Le Gemme Tygar. A scent I'd recognize anywhere.

A knock sounded, but barely three seconds later, my front door swung open. Only one friend had the nerve to treat my house like her own.

"Paige's here, so everybody get their shit together," she yelled from the foyer, her voice thick with attitude and barely contained worry.

I let out a shaky breath as Paige rushed in wearing Crocs, a bonnet, and a hoodie that said **SINCERELY, A BLACK GIRL WITH BOUNDARIES**. She didn't even bother taking it off. She yoked me up into a hug.

"Oh, baby..." she whispered, arms locking around me. "I got you. If don't nobody else got you, you know I do."

I pressed my face into her shoulder, letting myself be held for more than a second. Paige smelled like cocoa butter and lavender. It was comforting in the most unexpected way.

A moment later, the door opened again. Charity entered like a woman who didn't come to play—trench coat thrown over a sharp black jumpsuit, heels clicking against the marble. She didn't say a word at first. She just walked up to me, cupped my face, and gently kissed my forehead.

"I'm here," she murmured. "And I'm not leaving today."

Maya came right in behind her, soft and calm, wearing a long cardigan and carrying a leather-bound Bible that looked a hundred years old. In the other hand was a bag of essentials—water, ginger tea, tissues, lip balm, and holy oil.

She embraced me with both arms, slow and grounding. "We're going to get through this. You don't have to understand anything today or tomorrow. It's in God's timing. Just breathe."

All four of us walked into the living room together. It felt surreal to see my friends settling into the space I shared with Jahi. Although we built this house together, it never felt like mine, and I'd never entertained my loved ones here. I left that up to him.

I sat with my hands in my lap, staring at the envelope that still hadn't left my grip.

Maya noticed first. "Honey... what's that in your hand? Is that something from Jahi?"

I nodded slowly. "A private investigator brought it over this morning. He's the one who initially told me about the accident. He said Jahi mailed it to him a couple days ago. He said it was only supposed to be given to me if something happened to him."

Paige's eyebrows shot up. "See? Uh-uh. Nope. No. That sounds shady as hell. That's the type of shit husbands do in those damn Lifetime movies right before some shit is about to go down."

"Paige?!" Maya shot her a look.

"What? I'm just saying. It's giving true crime special."

Charity rested her hand on my knee. "Open it when you're ready, and not a second before. Don't rush."

I swallowed hard. "I'm scared," I admitted in a whisper. "What if this letter tells me he lied to me about everything? What if he was into something dangerous? What if someone killed him because of it? My brain is on overload right now. There's just too much going on."

Maya reached over, taking my hand. "Whatever it says, you're not reading it alone."

I exhaled slowly and tore into the envelope. Inside, Jahi's perfect handwriting filled the page. Neat, sharp...the way he wrote when he wanted to impress someone.

Nuri,

If you are reading this, then something I feared has happened. There is no easy way to tell you the truth. I've made hella mistakes that put us both in danger. Please know... you were never the target. But they will come for you because of me, and for that I hate myself.

My breath caught.

Charity leaned closer, whispering, "Oh hell."

I continued reading, eyes stinging.

I didn't cheat on you, nor was I suspicious of you. I was trying to keep you alive.

My heart was beating out of my chest. Maya whispered a prayer under her breath.

I've been followed for months. Someone has been watching us. I was approached by a man who told me I owed something I never received. Somebody set me up, and I still don't know who.

Paige inhaled sharply. "Damn..."

If Reid brought you this letter, then I didn't make it out. I need you to listen carefully: Do not trust anyone who comes asking questions about me. That means anyone—police, lawyers, hell, not even the coroner. Do not mention anything I told you... ever. And Nuri, don't open the safe until you are sure no one is watching you. Everything you need is inside. Everything I should've told you sooner.

My fingers trembled, and all the ladies had shocked looks on their faces. As tears came to the surface, my vision blurred. I blinked hard and kept reading.

There were pieces of me and my life I never shared with you, and for that, I'm sorry. Please understand it wasn't because you didn't deserve to know, but because I needed time to process the path God was taking me on. From the moment you entered my life, it propelled in a way I'd never imagined. Because of you, I got to experience a love I never thought I would. I went places and saw things I never dreamed of, and all I can say is thank you. I didn't deserve you, but I did love you.

I may not have done the right things all the

time, but please know I tried. I tried to be what everyone needed me to be. Please tell my parents I love them, and tell your parents I said ease up on you a little. They've always been too hard on you. I should have spoken up for you a long time ago. All this shit is my fault, and I'm owning it, but if you're reading this, it doesn't matter. Please forgive me for the danger I've caused. Be careful.

Jahi

I took the deepest breath imaginable. I couldn't believe what I'd just read.

"Nuri, that was some heavy shit," Paige muttered. "We need to hurry up and head to that damn safe because that letter didn't answer shit."

Charity groaned. "It sure as hell didn't. Here I was thinking he was about to spill some tea, and he served you piss. That joker was talking riddles. I never did like that about him. He never gave a straight answer to anyone. He always talked in metaphors like his ass was Jesus or somebody."

"Charity, have some respect. This man is dead and isn't here to defend himself," Maya stated.

"Exactly, Maya, which is what pisses me off even more. My girl is sitting over here scared, not knowing if someone will walk through that door at any second and snatch her ass up, and all his ass offered is 'I made some mistakes.' See, I know bullshit when I hear it. I'm in public relations, and I know when someone is avoiding questions. This is what I do for a living. I'm telling you... that was a master class in gaslighting. Anyway, let me not make this about me." She turned to me. "Nuri, are you okay? How did you feel about that bullshit you just read?"

"Honestly, Charity, the same way you do. This man knew his actions put him and me in danger and said nothing. He knew something was coming and didn't warn me. Why would he keep some shit like this from someone he claimed he loved? I'm so damn mad right now because it's clear that he didn't give a fuck about me."

The grief I felt was slowly turning into anger. I wanted so badly to believe he had my best interest at heart, but everything he'd done up until his death would say otherwise.

"Okay, Nuri," Paige interjected. "The best thing we can do is get to the safe and figure out what's really going on. He said that's where the answers are."

"Wait, wait, wait. The letter also said to be careful and make sure no one is watching her. We at least need to do a sweep of the house. Maybe look for cameras she didn't know existed," Maya offered.

"Girl, this is her damn house, and there is nobody here

but us. Why don't you make sure we are all protected and rub some of that oil on us? Then we can head to the safe with the whole armor of God on us," Paige chuckled.

"Hold on now. I play about a lot of things, Paige, but my God is not one of them. I will not sit here and let you make a mockery of Him."

"Maya, who said anything about making a mockery? I'm dead-ass serious. Girl, like Lil Boosie loves to say—I'm Southern Baptist. I know all about blessing oil. My granny would anoint our heads at least once a week when we were growing up. She said it would keep the evil away."

"Well, it obviously didn't work too well on you, considering you're standing here behaving like a heathen."

"Now hold on, you long denim skirt, tube sock wearing hei—" Paige snapped.

"Both of you, stop!" I shouted. "I can't take this shit right now. The last thing I need is the two of you arguing. There is bigger shit going on, in case y'all hadn't noticed."

"Nuri, you're right. I'm sorry. I know better than that, but you know how passionate I am about my God."

"I'm sorry too, big head. Please forgive us. I think we are all a little on edge after seeing that letter. I tell you what—how about I get in this kitchen, whip us up some breakfast and a couple of mimosas, and I'm positive we will all calm down. It's early in the morning, we've gotten bad news, and I don't know about the rest of you, but I am hungrier than a hostage."

"That sounds like a plan, Paige. Although, I'm not sure if I can eat right now. My nerves are shot, and my stomach is queasy."

"Queasy or not, I'm cooking, and you're going to eat," Paige commanded. "We cannot afford you passing out. Not on my watch."

As I sank back onto the couch, Charity came and put her head on my shoulder and whispered, "While Maya is anointing the house and Paige is cooking, we can go to the safe if you want. Just us. Look, I know you're scared, and I know this is hard for you, but you deserve answers. I don't want you torturing yourself with the whens and whys. Besides, not one thing in that safe can hurt you more than being left in the damn dark."

"I'm going to the safe, Charity, but I think it's best if I head down there by myself. I don't want you all involved with whatever shit he's gotten me into. Please don't argue with me about this. Let me do things the way that makes me feel the most comfortable. I hope you understand."

"I do," she responded. "You must do things your way, Nuri."

I stared at the ceiling, contemplating my next move, my chest growing tighter and tighter as each second passed.

Chapter Five

For the rest of the morning, the house felt crowded with more questions than answers. I moved through it like I was floating, half in my body and half somewhere my mind couldn't comprehend yet. Paige whipped up a five-star breakfast, and I forced myself to take a bite. Afterwards, Maya prayed softly in the corner, hands folded, eyes closed. Charity paced the floor, staring out the windows like she was waiting for reporters. Paige sat on the chaise and rocked back and forth like a mental patient ready to throw hands.

Every few minutes or so, my eyes drifted to the window. The street looked still, quiet, even normal, but I didn't know what normal was anymore. Not after last night. Not after the private investigator and damn sure not after the letter. I held Jahi's words in my hand like a stick of dynamite.

Don't open the safe.

Not yet.

Not until you're sure no one's watching you.

But how could I ever be sure? Especially knowing he had someone watching me for months and I had no idea. This was some bullshit.

Seeing the frustration on my face, Paige asked, "Where is the damn safe, Nuri? Is it in that damn forbidden office?"

"No," I shook my head slowly. "This one is different. Jahi had a private safe installed in the house about a year ago. Said it was for important documents, but I never saw the inside, and he was always changing the code."

Charity raised both brows. "A married man with a whole secret safe? Yeah, he was into some shit."

Maya gave her a look. "Charity, have a little couth."

"What? I'm telling the truth."

I rubbed my fingers through my hair. "I didn't care at the time. We were already pulling apart. I thought he was being controlling. Not hiding anything super important."

Maya's voice came in soft. "Where is it, honey?"

"If I'm being honest... I'd forgotten all about that thing until this shit started going down. It's somewhere in the basement. He had it recessed into the wall. You would never know it was there unless you knew exactly where to push."

Paige's eyes lit up. "Shidd, what are we waiting on? Let's go."

"No," I shook my head. "Just like I told Charity, I want to do it alone."

I stood up, heading to the safe room, when the doorbell rang. Paige stood first. "I'll get it."

"No," I whispered. "I need to."

I smoothed my shirt, wiped my eyes, and walked to the door slowly and cautiously. When I opened it, a man in a dark suit stood there.

"Detective?" I chirped.

"Yes, how did you know?" he questioned.

"I could tell from your posture. I've seen *The First 48* enough."

"I'm Detective Leo Dollars, Atlanta PD. I'm the lead investigator on your husband's crash. May I come in?"

My stomach flipped. *Don't trust anybody* rang in my ear. I stepped aside because refusing would only raise red flags.

"Ummm, sir, did you say your last name was Dollars?" Charity asked.

"I did indeed."

"Well damn. That is a pimp name if I've ever heard one. Is that the name your mama gave you or some shit you came up with on your own? Cause I've never heard that be someone's real last name."

He shot her a look. "I guess it's a first time for everything. Anyhow, hello ladies."

Paige muttered under her breath, "Here we go..."

"Listen, Detective. The police already came this morning. They told me all about the accident."

"Yes, ma'am. I'm aware, but they gave you the basics. I'm here for a different reason."

Maya shifted. "What reason?"

"There are... inconsistencies with your husband's crash."

"Inconsistencies?" I echoed. "Please explain."

Dollars nodded once. "We're not ruling out anything yet, but based on what we found... this may not have been an accident."

Charity sat up straight. "So you think he was murdered?"

"CHARITY," the other two snapped.

Dollars watched them quietly, then turned back to me. "I'm here because we found something that connects to you."

I blinked. "To me? What in the fuck are you referring to, officer, because I was home in my bed when this shit went down."

"Not like that, Mrs. Laurent." He reached into a folder and pulled out a photograph and held it up.

I could have sworn the room tilted. It was a half-burned picture of me leaving the Buckhead Ritz last night, walking toward my car. It was the same moment I noticed the black sedan. My knees felt so weak.

"Now why would he have that?" I asked Detective Dollars.

"That's what we are trying to figure out," he said. "Do you have any idea who might've taken this?"

The question made my mouth go dry. "Ummm, excuse me for a moment. Maya, can you please get me a bottled water from the fridge? I'm sorry, Detective. My nerves were already shot from getting the news about my husband, but this picture takes the cake."

Maya came back with the water. I took a swig and inhaled deeply.

"Someone was following me last night. That picture must have come from whoever it was. What I'm trying to figure out is how it got in my husband's possession, because I'm almost positive he had nothing to do with this person."

Maya whispered, "Lord..."

"We don't know, and that's what we are trying to figure out. Well, what about this?" He questioned before sliding another paper out of the folder.

This time it wasn't a photo. It was a name, handwritten and underlined twice.

"Do you know this person?"

My breath hitched in my throat because I did. Intimately and painfully. It was someone from my past I'd tried to forget. My voice cracked when I said the name aloud.

"Armani Fields."

All three of the girls looked at me sharply.

Charity's eyes widened. "Hold on... your ex, Armani? Armani Armani? Like before Jahi?"

"Oh, this is getting messy as hell," Maya muttered.

"I know we ain't cussing, Miss Almighty Church Mother," Paige snapped as she whipped her neck toward Maya.

Maya clutched her pearls, not realizing what had just come from her mouth.

But Detective Dollars wasn't done.

"This Armani character is not just someone from your past," he said quietly. "He's also the last person your husband called before he died."

The room fell silent. Dead silent. Chills flowed all through my body.

Because Armani was not just a chapter from my past. He was a door I had closed with force, and now it had swung wide open again.

Detective Dollars broke the silence with, "Mrs. Laurent, I've done some research on your husband, and I see that he was the man around town. He had his hands in a little bit of everything. I read that he was one of the big shots at Kinsley Pheonix Consortium. K.P.C. That's your parents' company, correct?" He raised a brow like he expected me to lie.

"Yes, and?" I said in a matter-of-fact tone.

"I was just making sure. I didn't mean anything by it. I was just letting you know that I was doing my research. I also discovered that he had a few run-ins with the law but was let off with a slap on the wrist, which isn't uncommon when a family has as much money as yours does. Word on the street was that he had a spending problem. Like buying properties just to have them, cars, hell, even that plane that's registered in his name. Do you know anything about that, Mrs. Laurent?"

"Detective One Dollar," Paige interrupted, "it sounds like you are assuming something about my girl here, and I can assure you she doesn't know shit and hasn't done shit. I've known her since high school, and I can vouch for her character."

"So can I," Charity blurted out. "If you came to check her out, then you are barking up the wrong tree. I suggest you get on up that road and investigate people that actually need to be investigated, because she's not the one. And if you have any more questions, we can get her lawyer on the phone. Besides, she's been through enough, and the day isn't even close to over." Charity stood up and put her hands on her hips.

"Listen, I'm sorry. You ladies are right," he uttered while rubbing the back of his neck and turning his attention back toward me. "I know today must be incredibly difficult for you, and I'm sure I didn't make it better by laying more on your plate. For that, I apologize. But I'm just trying to get ahead of this thing because whatever happened to your husband, we don't need it to happen to you too. That is what we are trying to prevent. I'm going to leave you with my card and get out of here for now, but I will be keeping in touch as the investigation continues. I see that you have a full support system with you, and I'm sure more will come. We are finished here for the day. Mrs. Laurent, once again, I am terribly sorry for your loss, and please call me if you need anything, and I do mean anything."

"Will do, Detective, and thank you for coming out and rattling my nerves even more. Good looking out."

He smiled, waved goodbye to the ladies, and made his way out the front door.

"Now wait a damn minute. What in the hell is Armani doing talking to your husband? Like I said earlier, this feels like some Lifetime kind of shit. Because what could those two possibly have to talk about? Armani hated Jahi from what I understood, and the feeling was mutual. That's it, Nuri. You have got to open that motherfucking safe, and I mean right now. If you want to go by yourself, fine, go. We will stay here and check the surroundings, but you need to take your ass there and see what was up. You need to see what the hell Jahi really had going on."

"I need you ladies to realize that I am not a child. I can think for myself, you know," I gritted. "Listen, I know you all love me and you are here for me, and I couldn't thank you enough, but I have family coming in soon, so I need to prepare. Plus, I know the county will probably be calling me shortly to view my husband's body, so I would like to be alone."

"What do you mean that you would like to be alone?" Charity questioned. "We are here for you, and we don't think that you should be here by yourself. It's not a matter of us trying to control you, but it's more of us trying to make sure that you're safe, especially with what that detective just laid on us."

"Us? Don't you mean what the detective just laid on me? You all will leave here and go back to your normal lives. I am the one stuck with this mess and trying to figure it out, and I am asking you all nicely to please just leave. Let me figure some things out alone. I know where every gun in this house is, and I will be OK, but I want you all to go."

Charity looked at Paige, and Paige looked at Maya.

"Ladies, we have to respect her decision. This is her house, and she has spoken. We've been here for a while, and she seems fine. She wants us to leave, so I think we should grab our things and go," Maya said.

"Maya, how are you gonna sit here and agree with her foolishness? It is clear she's out of her mind," Paige griped. "It's probably because of the stress, but don't cosign that shit. She doesn't need to be alone, and I don't give a damn what she says."

"That's how you feel, Paige," Maya uttered. "That isn't how she feels, and this is her house. You two can sit here and figure it out, but I'm a lady, and a lady always knows when to bow out gracefully." Maya turned to me and smiled. "I'm leaving, sweetheart. I love you, and call me if you need anything," she said before grabbing her things and heading toward the front door.

I stood there, looking at Paige and Charity, hoping they would follow suit, but these two were stubborn as mules.

"Who in the hell am I going to have to fight to get you two to leave? I am serious. I want you both gone so I can think clearly without interruption."

"Well fuck it then. We will leave, but don't call us

crying when your mean-ass Mama shows up and starts trying to run things," Charity said as she walked over to me and planted a kiss on my cheek.

"She's right. Don't call me either because I plan on being three sheets in the wind by noon. But do call me and tell me what was in that muthafucking safe," Paige chuckled as she hugged my cheek.

"Bye, bitch," they said in unison as they sashayed out the door.

Chapter Six

I exhaled as I stood at the window watching them all drive away. I closed the gate and decided I wouldn't open it again until Jahi's parents arrived. I hadn't heard back from them, and I wasn't sure when or what time they'd show up, but they would have to get buzzed through like everyone else. As soon as the house went quiet, I stood alone at the top of the basement steps with Jahi's letter folded tight in my hand.

Don't open the safe until you're sure no one is watching.

I didn't know how to be sure of that, but I wasn't waiting anymore. The basement lights flickered on as I descended, concrete rigid and cool beneath my bare feet. This was Jahi's domain...entertainment, storage, archived files, things meant to be forgotten. He'd had the safe installed during a time when the company was at its highest. The safe was tucked behind a custom wall panel disguised as shelving. I remembered laughing when he showed it to me, teasing him about being so extra.

Now my hands trembled as I pressed around the wall to find the exact spot he once showed me. The panel released with a soft click. There it was. Steel. Matte black and unassuming. I stared at the keypad, my pulse loud in my ears. Jahi had always used numbers that meant something to him. Dates. Codes. Memory triggers. I tried his birthday first. Nothing. Then my birthday, nothing once again. Then I remembered the night he came home nervous and shaken, saying something had "gone wrong at work." I'd written the date in my journal because I'd never seen him behave that way..

Nervously, I entered the numbers and the safe unlocked. Bingo, we've got action. I stepped back like it might explode. Inside were neatly stacked folders, flash drives, a leather-bound notebook, and a slim metal box with a lock. Everything was labeled and organized. Just like him.

Jahi had been preparing. I pulled out the first folder.

KINSLEY PHEONIX CONSORTIUM – CONFIDENTIAL

My parents' company. I immediately felt nauseous. Inside were financial statements, not the versions presented to investors, but raw numbers. Offshore transfers, shell accounts layered three and four companies deep. Money moved through international holdings I'd never heard of. Amounts so large they didn't feel real. Nothing about this shit looked legit. My head throbbed as I flipped page after page. There were handwritten notes in Jahi's margin.

This account shouldn't exist. Someone is skimming. Board unaware or pretending to be. I'm narrowing down and I think I'm close.

I opened the next folder.

GREYSTONE PROJECT

The name meant nothing to me until I saw the contracts. Private land acquisitions tied to redevelopment zones that hadn't been approved. Properties that were bought quietly and cheaply then rezoned months later for a passive profit. Political names appeared repeatedly...city officials, board members, donors. People that my husband sat across from daily in boardrooms. Bribes that were disguised as "consulting fees." I covered my mouth. This shit wasn't just unethical. This was criminal. Another folder.

SURVEILLANCE AND COUNTERMEASURES

My heart almost stopped. Photos slid out, grainy and time-stamped. Me, leaving charity galas, meeting friends, or sitting alone in cafés. Dates stretched months back. Jahi hadn't just been protecting me; he'd been documenting something. A Post-it was smacked on the front that read: *She is being watched by someone else. Not us.*

This shit was truly overwhelming, and I was nowhere near done. I dropped to the floor on my knees and sat back to take it all in. Everyone around me was into some shit they shouldn't have been, and I had no choice but to look at everyone like a suspect.

I stood back up and started back plundering. It was creepy as hell in the basement, and I wanted to get out ASAP. The flash drives came next. I didn't plug them in, not yet. Jahi had been clear about that kind of thing. Instead, I opened the leather notebook. His handwriting filled every page. Pages of timelines along with names and warnings. He'd suspected someone inside Kinsley Pheonix Consortium was moving money through Greystone, setting him up to take the fall. He'd started asking questions quietly and carefully, but obviously not carefully enough.

The last page stopped me in my tracks.

If something happens to me, it wasn't an accident. Someone wanted what I had. I don't know whether they wanted information, or my wife.

My breathing was shallow as I reached for the last metal box. It required a key, and I already knew where the key was. I was unknowingly wearing it around my neck every day. A simple gold chain Jahi had given me years ago. He told me it was "the key to his heart."

I looked over my shoulder as I unlocked the box. Inside was a single document. A revised trust naming me as the beneficiary, successor authority, and emergency control clause. Jahi had transferred access, not ownership, but control of specific K.P.C. accounts to me in the event of his death. Not only was he protecting me, but he was also positioning me. I sat there on the cold floor, the truth settling into my bones. My husband didn't die because he was careless. He died because he knew too much. And now, so did I.

I heard a faint noise upstairs. Although I knew my house was empty... I got spooked. I snapped the safe shut and replaced the panel, my heart pounding so hard that it could be heard outside my body. And just like that, I was no longer just the grieving wife. I was also a threat.

Chapter Seven

With that harsh realization sitting heavy on my chest, I ran back upstairs and sat on my couch. I wanted someone to come save me and make all this weird shit go away. But I knew no one was coming. The very man I thought didn't love me anymore because he'd become cold and distant was the only one who seemed to have my best interest at heart. I just wish I would have known, because I was almost positive that he lightweight hated me.

Now he was gone, and whatever protection he offered me before was gone right along with him. I had to protect myself. I sat around for the rest of the day trying to figure out what I'd just seen and what it meant for my near future. I was a smart girl, but a lot of what I saw was company jargon. He may as well have been writing in hieroglyphics because some of the things he mentioned were completely foreign to me.

I grabbed my laptop and began researching. I could have called Charity, but that would have meant explaining what I found, and I wasn't about to do that. While researching, my girls blew my phone up repeatedly. Their calls went unanswered, as well as my parents'. I didn't feel like talking or explaining shit to anyone. They were going to be nosy and I couldn't involve them in my findings. I sent them all a text message telling them I was okay, but I needed time to process. When I was ready, I'd reach out. Paige had a full five-course Italian dinner delivered to my house. If she didn't do anything else, she was going to make sure I was fed.

Later that evening, right before dusk, I was alerted of Mr. Mercer at the gate. I opened it to let him in. Exiting his car, he stood on the porch. He didn't knock. He rang the doorbell once, then waited. When I opened the door, his eyes scanned past me, automatically cataloging windows, corners, and shadows.

"You opened it," he said, but it wasn't a question.

I stepped aside. "You knew I would."

He gave a quick nod and walked in, removing his jacket like he planned to stay a while.

"If he trusted you with that letter, that must mean I can trust you too. You must have been good at your job?"

"Apparently too good," he smirked. "I'm sure now that you've cracked that safe open, there's no way you can go back to pretending."

"Not a chance in hell," I admitted. "At this point, that would be careless and stupid, and I'm neither."

We sat at the kitchen island. I slid the folders toward him without ceremony. Reid didn't react, just flipped through them with the quiet efficiency of someone who was used to seeing the worst of the worst.

"This is bad," he said finally. "But it's not messy bad. It's organized bad."

"You're telling me," I quipped.

He drew in a long breath. "That's not it, though. I've got something else I think I should share with you."

"Go ahead and lay it on me. It can't be as bad as this."

He leaned back, eyes landing on the ceiling for a moment. "Your husband wasn't just working for your parents' company. He was also running numbers. Bookmaking, but not just with anyone. I'm talking high-dollar, quiet, corporate types—politicians, athletes, developers... people who don't want their habits public."

My stomach twisted in knots. "That doesn't make sense because Jahi hated gambling."

"He hated losing control," Reid corrected. "That's why he was good at it. Jahi's side operation gave him leverage—information and liquidity. But it also put him on a short leash with dangerous people."

"So you're saying he was a bookie," I said slowly, "and a loan shark."

Reid nodded. "He fronted money too. Short-term. High interest. The kind of loans that could ruin lives if they went unpaid."

"Who owed him?"

Reid met my eyes. "That's the problem. Damn near everybody owed him."

I swallowed hard.

"And Armani?" I asked. "Why was his name in the safe, and why was he the last person my husband talked to?"

Reid's jaw tightened. "Well, that one's personal."

I felt the air leave my lungs. "Armani was my ex. Years before Jahi."

"I know," Reid said. "What you didn't know is that Armani started running collections for Jahi."

I cracked my knuckles. "Ummm, are you sure? Because Armani doesn't have the discipline for that."

"He didn't at first," Reid muttered. "He learned quickly, though. See, Armani also moved in elite circles—charity events, private parties. Same rooms as K.P.C.

investors. Jahi used him as a bridge...someone who could move unnoticed. Everyone knew who Jahi was, who he worked for, and what his goals were. Nobody really knew shit about Armani. Besides your parents, of course, and they didn't care what was happening as long as the money continued to flow into their pockets."

I could feel bile rising in my throat. "So Armani wasn't just an ex popping back up...he was part of Jahi's world."

"Yes," Reid stated. "And that's where things went sideways."

I stood and paced, my thoughts spiraling. "Let me guess—Armani fucked something up."

Reid didn't answer immediately.

"He fucked up when he started borrowing from Jahi," Reid finally said. "Small at first, then bigger. He racked up quite a tab, and when he couldn't pay, he started selling information and wolf tickets."

"Information about what?"

Reid looked me square in the eye. "About you. About K.P.C. About what he'd heard about Greystone...anything that would cause Jahi to worry."

"That sneaky, low-down, dirty muthafucka. So you're telling me he used me as currency."

"Yes."

"I don't understand how. I hadn't spoken to him in years, and it's not shit he could've told anyone about my husband that I would've believed. Armani is the grimiest son of a bitch I've ever met. He lies for sport. Jahi didn't have to worry when it came to him. After I closed the door on him, I tried to nail that bitch shut."

"I guess Jahi didn't trust that Armani couldn't get to you. Just your name flowing from Armani's lips pissed him off."

"Let me ask you something, Reid," I said as I snacked on a breadstick. "How do you know all this information? Obviously, Jahi trusted you in a lot of ways, but what made him trust you enough to explain the inner workings of his criminal activities?"

"Jahi wasn't just someone I worked for. We were good friends at one time. We went to Morehouse together. Played ball together. We forged a friendship, but after we graduated, we kind of lost touch. I showed up as a plus-one to a charity event, and there he was—standing on stage being auctioned off like cattle."

"So you knew him before the glitz and glamour?"

"I did. Plus, I think he could tell that I wasn't impressed by any of that. None of it phased me...not his money, clothes, cars, or the amount of women he could potentially pull. I could tell he was surrounded by nothing but yes-men, and that isn't me. I won't kiss anyone's ass no matter how much money they make."

I looked into his eyes and could tell he was a no-nonsense kind of man. So I believed him.

He continued. "I think that's what impressed him the most. Once he stepped off that stage, we dapped it up and started catching up. He told me all the things he'd accomplished, and I told him the same. I told him that day that I owned a P.I. firm. About three weeks later, I got a call from him out of the blue asking for my help. I met him at one of his investment properties, and he told me everything. That brother had some major things to get off his chest. The first thing he mentioned was you. Then immediately after...his bookie endeavors. I honestly knew nothing about the internal issues with the company until now. It doesn't surprise me one bit. Greed is common in places like that."

"Yes, it is, which is why I wanted no parts of my parents' company. They begged me to come work for them, but I went in my own direction. That's what was best for me. Otherwise, I'd be in prison and doomed to hell by now," I shrugged.

His head tilted to the side with confusion. "And what makes you say that?"

"Because I would've whooped my mother's ass by now," I chuckled. "We don't have the best relationship. I'm not sure if Jahi mentioned that to you or not, but yeah. Apparently, my mom can't stand my ass. It's been like that since I was a child, and I don't know why. I'm at the age where I don't give a damn. It annoys me, but it no longer hurts me."

"From what I understood, Jahi and your parents had a great relationship."

"You're right. Jahi had a great relationship with them. Not Nuri."

He searched my face, seemingly looking for hurt, but by this time I was over feelings. I was growing numb by the second.

"Speaking of your parents," he said, "did he say how they fell into all this?"

Reid exhaled slowly. "They knew something wasn't clean. They just didn't know how dirty."

I laughed, but wasn't shit funny. "That sounds like my mother."

"Jahi was trying to get out," Reid said. "He planned to shut down the book, call in debts, and expose Greystone internally. He thought if he cleaned his hands, the heat would die down."

"And instead?" I whispered.

"He became the liability."

I sank back into my chair. "So there wasn't just one reason why someone would want to get rid of my husband."

"No," Reid said quietly. "There were many."

Think about it, Nuri. K.P.C.'s internal theft. Then you had Greystone's corruption. Borrowers who didn't want to pay. And Armani trying to save himself.

"And me?" I asked. "Why am I still breathing?"

Reid's eyes softened. "Because they aren't sure what you know—or if you know anything at all. And because killing you would be too loud."

I nodded slowly. "But that won't last too much longer, will it?"

"No, it won't," he said, his head down.

Silence filled the room.

Finally, I asked the question I'd been avoiding.

"Did Armani have anything to do with Jahi's death?"

Reid held my gaze. "I don't think he did it himself."

"But?" I whispered.

"But he might've made it possible."

His words sat heavy in my chest. Jahi hadn't just been surrounded by danger. He'd been drowning in it, and now every secret he carried was spilling into my lap.

Reid stood, slipping his jacket back on. "Nuri, you need to decide who you're going to be in this."

I looked up at him. "Meaning?"

"Pawn," he said evenly. "Or player."

I didn't hesitate. "Oh baby, you best believe I'm going to be the player."

Reid nodded once. "Good. Then your next move is confronting Armani before someone else does."

My pulse quickened. "And after that?"

Reid's expression darkened. "After that, we find out how far K.P.C. is willing to go to protect itself."

I watched him walk toward the door, my life no longer recognizable. Jahi hadn't just left me grief...he left me a war.

Chapter Eight

I waited until midnight to call Armani. Not because I was afraid, but because that's when the city softened and guards were usually let down. He answered on the first ring.

"Armani Phillips answering."

"Armani... this is Nuri."

"Nuri," he said it like my name had been sitting on his tongue all day. "Well, what do I owe the pleasure? Oh... before we go any further, let me offer you my sincerest condolences. I am terribly sorry for your loss. Are you okay?"

I closed my eyes. "Don't do that."

"Do what?"

"Act like you care."

He laughed softly. Too softly. "Baby, I've always cared. I never stopped."

That word *baby* almost dragged me backwards. To rooftop nights. To heat rising off the Atlanta pavement. To Armani with his shiny golden smile, quick hands and a big dick.

"Nuri, do you remember when you would scream my name so loud that I'd have to stuff your mouth with my shirt? Or what about that time when we were in Cabo and we made love in the ocean and I got bit on the ass by Lord knows what. I was down for the count for some days, but the experience was worth it. I wouldn't trade those memories for the world."

"Are you fucking serious right now? You are disrespectful as hell. My husband's head isn't even cold yet. Stop reminiscing, you asshole. I didn't call for nostalgia."

"But nostalgia is all we have," he replied. "You remember Miami? That suite with the—"

"Did you have anything to do with my husband's death?" I asked coldly.

The silence on the other end was sharp.

Then he sighed. "Straight to business, huh. You always hated foreplay."

My jaw tightened. "Correction… I hated foreplay from you. You weren't as good at it as you thought. Now, answer me."

"I didn't kill Jahi," Armani said finally. "If that's what you're asking."

"That's not what I asked."

Another long pause. Longer this time.

"You married a dangerous man," he said carefully. "Danger doesn't come from just one direction."

"So that's a yes?"

"It's an I don't know what you want me to say."

"You always knew exactly what to say," I snapped. "That was your gift."

"And you loved me for it," he shot back. "Until you didn't."

I exhaled slowly. "If you know something, Armani—"

"I know enough to tell you this," he interrupted. "Whatever Jahi was mixed up in, you were never supposed to be part of it."

"But I am now?"

"Yes, you are."

I gripped the phone. "Were you there?"

"I was around," he said. "Atlanta's a small city when money's involved."

"That's not an answer."

"You never liked straight lines," he murmured. "You liked curves, remember. Like the one in my dick."

I hung up on him before I threw the phone across the room.

The next morning, I called Reid and the girls and asked them to meet me at the county. We went to see what was left of my husband. The room was too white. Too quiet. Jahi appeared smaller than what I remembered. Most of his body was burned, and it pained me to see him like that. I lowered myself down to him.

"Why couldn't you have just stayed home with me, my love? Who were you going to meet?"

I held his hand. None of this felt real. "I'm so sorry this happened to you. You didn't deserve to go out like this."

I kissed his cheek, said my final goodbyes, and tearfully left the building with my girls and Reid by my side.

We walked out of the county examiner's office like four women who had just survived something we did not consent to. My eyes were swollen. My head hurt. My soul felt like it needed a nap and a therapist. All I wanted was my couch, my robe, and darkness.

Reid motioned for me to come to him and pulled me to the side. "I know that was hard for you, but it's over. Are you okay?" he asked in the sincerest voice.

"No, but I will be. I'm just going to head home and drown myself in a bottle of wine. I'll be fine. I want to thank you so much for coming. I know he was your boss and friend, and I figured you'd want to see him one last time as well. In case you didn't guess, it's going to be a closed casket."

"Thank you for allowing me to be here. I'm honored, and I appreciate you thinking of me. Listen, your girls are looking at me crazy, so I'm going to head on out. Call me if you need anything." He hugged me and waved goodbye to the ladies.

I walked back over to the group. "I'm going home," I announced in the parking lot.

Paige stopped walking.

Not slowed or hesitated. But stopped. She turned around slowly, her face contorted. I just knew she was going to be on some bullshit.

"No, you're not."

I blinked. "I beg your pardon?"

"You just saw your husband in a metal meat drawer," she said calmly. "If you go home right now, you're going to cry, overthink, and start rewriting your marriage like it was a Terry McMillan novel."

"I feel judged."

"You should," she replied. "We're going to brunch."

Maya gasped like Paige had suggested armed robbery. "Paige... that feels disrespectful."

Charity tilted her head. "Yes, it's morally questionable but emotionally necessary. She'll be okay. It's not like we are dragging her off to meet her maker."

"I'm not hungry," I declared.

Paige waved that away. “Grief will tell you a lie. Pancakes won’t.”

The restaurant was loud, bright, and offensively cheerful. We slid into a booth, grabbing menus as we settled in. Paige immediately ordered mimosas for the table without asking.

Maya whispered, “I don’t think I should be drinking.”

Paige leaned in. “Baby, after today, Jesus understands.”

Charity took a sip and sighed. “Okay... now that we’re seated and breathing... can we talk about how fine that man was?”

Maya nearly dropped her menu. “CHARITY.”

“What?” Charity said. “I’m alive. I have eyes. I was thinking the whole time, ‘Where in the hell does she know him from?’ You’d never mentioned a Reid before.”

I snorted before I could stop myself. “I saw the way y’all were looking at him when he walked up. Paige, I just knew you were going to say something crazy, but I was so glad you didn’t. He worked for Jahi and was a good friend to him. I wanted him to be there too.”

Paige leaned back, lips curling into a grin. “No, because why did nobody warn me he was that fine?”

Maya squeezed her eyes shut. “This is not the time.”

“This is exactly the time,” Paige argued. “We just stared death in the face. Let us stare at something beautiful. That man would be considered fine on every continent. His skin was so smooth. He must be using that damn Korean skincare that they're peddling on TikTok every five damn minutes."

Charity cackled and nodded her head in agreement.

"He's a tall glass of dark chocolate milk," Paige continued. "He looks like he's almost seven feet tall, but if I had to guess, I would say six foot six. He doesn't look like he has an ounce of body fat on him. Pure muscle, which means pure strength. I could melt into those arms of his, and did you see his eyes? His eyes were gorgeous. My mama used to call those bedroom eyes."

Charity nodded thoughtfully. "That man looks like he drinks his coffee black, never raises his voice, and would absolutely ruin someone's life if necessary."

Paige offered, "Shidd, I've been waiting to find somebody to fuck my life up over."

The whole table erupted in laughter, including the table next to us.

Maya stared at us like she was reconsidering her friendships. "You all are unbelievable."

Paige wasn't done. "I'm just saying... he's got that quiet, 'I don't talk much but I know things' face. Broad shoulders. Calm, kind eyes, and that bulge in his pants says his shoe size is at least a thirteen."

Charity added, "The kind of fine that doesn't flirt. You

just look up one day and he has a key, bought you a dog, and has his mail coming to your house."

I cackled as I shook my head. "Y'all are ridiculous."

Paige pointed at me. "Don't lie. You noticed."

I sighed. "Okay. Yes. He's... offensively handsome. That I can agree on."

Charity leaned forward. "Define offensively."

I thought about it for a second. "Like... he looks like he could stand in a doorway and make bad decisions rethink themselves."

Paige hit the table. "THAT'S IT. That's the exact description I was looking for."

Maya covered her face. "I'm begging you to stop. Can we please just go somewhere one time and act like we've got some sense?"

The waiter came by, clearly confused by our energy. "Is everything okay here?"

Paige smiled sweetly. "We're grieving and horny, but in a respectful way."

The waiter blinked. "I'll... give y'all a minute."

When he walked away, we hollered and cut up, cackling. For a few minutes, we laughed. Real laughter. The kind that startled me because I didn't know I still had it in me. Paige told a story she absolutely should not have. Charity added commentary. Maya shook her head the entire time but smiled anyway.

And for just a moment, the heaviness lifted. It didn't erase anything, and it didn't fix the ache. But it reminded me I was still here. Still human. Still capable of laughing at inappropriate times with women who loved me enough to drag me to brunch.

And honestly?

That felt like a small miracle.

SHORTLY AFTER I arrived back home, my parents arrived, and his parents followed. They were grief stricken, stunned, and still in disbelief.

His parents and I made the arrangements. I took a backseat and let them do what they felt. I knew they would do my husband justice. In the end, everyone was pleased.

By week's end, flowers filled my house. Expensive ones. Orchids, lilies, white roses from people I didn't recognize or know. Cards came with no return addresses, and the guests came in waves. Women were crying, some crying too damn hard for my liking, while the men were watching closely. The reporters lingered outside my gate trying to get a shot of Jahi's grieving widow. Cameras were pointed like weapons. It was too much. I completely stopped opening the door myself. By the time the funeral came, I felt hollow.

The service was beautiful. Painfully so. Over nine

hundred people came to show their respects. His parents arranged a stellar gospel choir. A polished eulogy talked about Jahi's brilliance, his generosity, and his vision. His friends and colleagues spoke of him like he belonged to the city, like Atlanta itself had lost a son. And then there were the women. One after another, dressed impeccably with tears streaking their faces, as if they clutched tissues and memories that I didn't have access to. They wept like his lovers. They had to pull one of them from the casket.

I didn't study them too long because the men unsettled me more. They weren't crying. Most of them didn't even seem sad. They were watchful. Every move I made felt measured.

At the burial, as the casket lowered into the earth, I felt it. That prickle at the back of my neck. Someone was staring at me. Watching me. I scanned the crowd, and there just beyond the tree line, a man stood apart, face clearly showing. We locked eyes. He didn't look away when I noticed him. I blinked just for a second, and he was gone.

After saying our final goodbyes, we all headed back to the church for the repast. The last thing I wanted to do was eat fried chicken, green beans, potato salad, and that dry ass roll that always seemed to be served after funerals. I somberly walked into the building, surprised to find KPC had the food catered. The menu consisted of all of Jahi's favorite foods. Lobster tails, caviar, prime rib, wagyu steaks, lamb chops, creamed truffle mashed potatoes, prosciutto wrapped persimmons with goat cheese, lobster mac and cheese, and so much more. It was ridiculous. Even in death, he had to do it big.

I was directed to sit up front. That way, people had easy access to come express their sorrows and condolences, which was exactly what I wanted to avoid. I wasn't like my husband. I hated attention, and I hated it even more if it was forced. Before the attendees could get started, I headed to the restroom. I relieved myself, and just as I began to wash my hands, a beautiful woman stepped out of the stall.

"Nuri," she called out. "Hi, I'm Shantel," she said as she raised her hand for me to shake.

Shantel was a gorgeous, thick redbone with a pixie cut. She had big breasts that sat up like two grapefruits on her chest, a tiny waist, and a clearly sculpted, silicone filled ass. After giving her a once over, I grabbed a paper towel, dried my hands, then shook hers.

"Ummm, I know most would say this isn't the time or the place, but I just thought you—"

"Let me stop you right there," I quipped, cutting her off mid sentence. "If you are about to tell me my husband was fucking on you, you can keep that information to yourself. He and his dick are dead, and I really don't give a damn. None of that shit matters now, and me knowing won't change anything. Just so you are aware, all good people would have definitely told you this wasn't the time or the place. Not just some. Now please get the fuck out my face and go back out there and eat your piece of steak and your scoop of potatoes and go the fuck home."

She glanced in the mirror, applied more lipstick, smacked her lips, and trekked out the bathroom. Following behind her, I headed back to my table. Maya, Paige, and Charity were waiting for me. They could see the look on my face as I placed my purse down before sitting.

"I know we just buried your husband, but why does it look like you've been sucking on lemons? What's wrong? You were fine a minute ago," Paige asked.

"I would tell you all, but I know how you all would react. I want to keep the peace and get home without tearing this place up."

"Well, you've got to tell us now. You can't say shit like that and expect us not to want to know," Charity muttered.

"I'll tell you, but I won't tell you who. Some woman came to me while I was in the bathroom. She thought she was about to have a woman to woman talk, and I cut her right the fuck off."

"Oh my Jesus," Maya whispered under her breath.

"Woman to woman like, 'Hey, I was fucking your

man?'" Paige asked. Her forehead was tight. That was never a good sign.

"Yes, but don't worry. I'm good. That shit meant nothing to me. My name is on all the bank accounts and the deeds. There is nothing else I'm concerned about. Besides, he's dead. It's not like I can confront him, so I'll take her almost confession with a grain of salt."

Paige tried to whisper but got louder with each word. "I know you fucking lying. Which bitch in here had the nerve to walk up to you minutes after you buried YOUR HUSBAND and try to confess some shit? Point her out," she yelled as she looked around for guilty faces.

"I'm not doing that. Please stop. Like I said, it doesn't matter."

Just as I convinced Paige to calm down, the elders began to approach me. They laid hands, prayed for me, and offered their sincerest condolences. I was tired of condolences and wanted nothing more than to get away from everyone. By the time I left, I was mentally drained and wanted to shut the world out.

After it was all over, our parents prepared to leave. We shared hugs, made promises, and grief lingered while wrapped in designer coats.

The house felt too big once they were gone, but I was glad for the silence. I tried to settle back into what was normal for me, but that was impossible, especially still not knowing who killed my husband.

One night, a few weeks later, I hopped up and decided to be productive. I opened the mail I'd been avoiding for weeks, and there it was. A letter from the insurance company. I read it once. Then again. Then a third time. The numbers stared back at me, obscene and unrealistic. A payout so large it didn't feel like relief. It felt like a burden.

I sank into a chair, the weight of it pressing down on my chest. Jahi hadn't just left me secrets. He'd left me money, and lots of it. And in the world I lived in, money didn't mean safety. It meant attention. We were already well off and lived a life of luxury, but we were wealthy with assets. Now I was wealthy with cold hard cash.

I made the decision right then and there. No one would know the amount. It was a number I'd take to my grave with me. If this information were to get out, I could be sure that whoever killed my husband would be gunning for me next.

Chapter Nine

I kept my head down and chin up. I continued moving through life the best way I knew how. Things were relatively quiet, and I was pleased with that, but I never stopped looking over my shoulder. I knew it was only a matter of time before someone came lurking. Until that moment, I would mind the business that paid me. Once the swelling went down, I asked Paige, Charity, and Maya if they would accompany me to Bali. I wanted to get away. I needed peace, tranquility, and understanding. Leaving behind the winter in Atlanta, I took my husband's private jet, and we were off for two weeks of relaxation and fun in the sun. We left 4 uptight, rigid ass females but returned to Atlanta wiser, grateful, and ready to face whatever was thrown at us.

That was until Armani showed up. Not announced,

not invited... just there. I knew it was on some bullshit before I opened the door. Some instincts don't fade; they sharpen. Through the security camera, I saw him standing just off center, like he didn't want to be fully captured. He was wearing a dark suit, no tie. Same confident stillness that used to make women flock to him without realizing it.

I opened the door anyway. Gun at my side.

"Nuri," he said softly, like we were alone in the world instead of surrounded by greed, cameras, and grief.

"Ummm, did you jump my damn gate?"

I peeked outside to make sure I hadn't left it open. It was closed.

"Girl, I'm a reformed thug. Ain't no gate stopping me, and you already know this."

"You have a lot of fucking nerve coming here and uninvited at that."

He smiled, that familiar, dangerous grin. "Now you know you've gotta have big balls to move the way I move."

I stepped back, stretching wide so my gun was visible and letting him in despite myself. The house felt smaller the minute he stepped across the threshold.

"You shouldn't be here," I said, closing the door.

"And you shouldn't be alone, yet here we are. Oh, and I see your little gun. You can put that away though. You should know I would never do anything to hurt you, Nuri."

I folded my arms. "Say what you came to say, Armani, because I don't have time to deal with dumb shit."

He glanced around, eyes lingering on the black framed photos, the funeral programs still neatly stacked on the table. "You buried him beautifully."

"I know you didn't darken my doorstep just to tell me that."

He finally looked at me... really looked. "You look different."

I scoffed. "Time does that. So does grief."

"No," he said quietly. "Truth does."

The air between us seemed to disappear.

"I heard you went to see him after the accident. Why would you want to see him like that?"

"What does it matter to you? That's not your damn business."

"Everything that touches you is my business. It has always been, and it will always be."

I laughed once, sharp. "That's exactly why I left you. You wanted to control my every move but wanted to run the streets like I didn't exist."

He stepped closer. Not touching. Armani had always known the power of personal space.

"You talk that shit, Nuri. But we were fire. Before money. Before all the expectations. Before you decided you wanted a man who looked safe."

“I wanted peace,” I snapped. “And you never offered that.”

“Neither did Jahi. He just made his chaos look better than mine, but it was chaos, nonetheless.”

His name rolling off Armani’s lips infuriated me.

“Watch your mouth.”

“Or what?” Armani asked softly as he took a step towards me.

I felt it then... the old pull I tried to avoid. The kind that made logic insignificant. Armani had been my first real recklessness. My first true love. He was the one that taught me desire never asked permission from anyone.

“Seriously, why are you here?”

His expression shifted, and his tone dropped. “Because things are moving.”

“Things like what? Stop beating around the bush and tell me what the fuck is happening?”

“The payout,” he said. “The book. The people who don’t know what you know — and the people who think you know more than you do.”

“I don’t know what you’re talking about. I don’t know shit.”

“Yeah, you may have others fooled, but I know you. Besides, Jahi looked like the type of man who told his woman everything. I bet he pillow talked for hours,” he said smugly.

"Like I said, I don't know shit. So, is that why you're here? To warn me?"

"I came to see which version of you I would get since he's gone. The girl who once trusted me with her life... or the woman who married him."

"First of all, I was stupid for trusting you back then, and I would be dumb as hell to trust you now. Answer me something and no bullshit or double talking." He held my gaze. "Did you help get my husband killed?"

Silence. It wasn't the awkward kind but the deliberate kind.

"I didn't save him."

I inhaled and exhaled deeply. "My God, Armani, talking to you is fucking infuriating. That was a yes or no question. What kind of answer is, 'I didn't save him?'"

"It's the only one I can give you and still sleep at night."

I shook my head slowly. "You always did that. Talk around the truth like it owed you something. You and Jahi had that in common."

"And you always filled in the blanks with that brilliant mind of yours. That's what makes you dangerous."

"Dangerous to who?"

"To the men who don't really know you. The ones that see that beautiful face of yours and think you are soft."

"Oh, you mean men like you? Because if I recall correctly… that's exactly what you did. You saw a beautiful young girl with the world at her fingertips. Someone you thought you could mishandle and would take whatever you dished out. I showed your ass, didn't I?" I snapped.

For a moment, neither of us moved. Then Armani reached into his jacket and pulled out a folded piece of paper.

"I don't want to argue, and I'm not trying to dredge up the past and piss you off. I've got something for you. No one knows about this, and if I didn't care about you, neither would you."

"What is it?"

"A name and a location."

My voice dropped. "What do I need this for?"

His jaw tightened. "You're being watched, Nuri. Not to hurt you. Not yet, anyway."

"Then why?"

"Because you're the last loose end. And because your man had major bread. Or it at least looked like he did. I'm sure you know money like yours can easily turn curiosity into obsession."

I finally took the paper. "If this blows back on you, don't come looking for me."

He flashed a slick smile my way. "I'll always come looking for you."

"Don't," I warned.

He stepped toward the door, then paused. "For what it's worth... if I could change one thing, it wouldn't be how this ends because I know you're gonna be good."

"Well, what would it be, Mani?"

"How we began."

The door closed behind him, and I unfolded the paper. A photograph dropped to the floor. It was the man I'd locked eyes with at the burial. Along with the photograph, there was a name, address, and the sinking realization that Armani wasn't the most dangerous man circling me. He was just the one who still knew how to get close.

Chapter Ten

I stared at the paper for a long time.

Armani's handwriting was unmistakable, slanted, confident, like he expected the world to bend around it. A name and address written in bold letters. An invitation to go looking for trouble under the guise of getting answers. Fuck that.

I folded it once, then again, and dropped it straight into the trash. No fire or dramatics, just finality. For the first time since Jahi died, I didn't feel reactive. Whatever bullshit that was circling me wanted movement, panic, or curiosity. I wasn't giving it shit, and I sure as hell wasn't about to chase shadows or let men with secrets and motives turn me into bait. For all I knew, Armani or one of the guilty coworkers had hired him to snuff me out.

If someone wanted me gone, they were going to have

to come to me, and I wouldn't be an easy win. That's when I called Reid and told him I needed his help. He arrived within the hour. No questions. No hesitation. Just quiet efficiency and eyes that missed nothing.

He walked through my house like it was already his. He checked the perimeter, reviewed camera angles, adjusted lighting, locked doors I didn't even realize were unlocked.

"You're serious," he said finally.

"Hell yes, I'm serious. I'm done being brave," I replied. "I want to be alive. Damn all that other shit, and I'll pay you whatever you ask to stay with me around the clock. Money is not an object."

Reid nodded. "Then from now on, you don't go anywhere alone, and don't ever say money isn't an object to anyone else. Money is half the reason why we are here."

"I just need you to watch my back just like you watched Jahi's. This isn't a Whitney and Kevin situation, and it should be easier than what my husband had you doing. This shit should be a cakewalk for you. I'm willing to do what you say, but I didn't agree to house arrest."

Calmly, he muttered, "But you did. You agreed the second you asked me for help. Since you didn't read the fine print, let me tell you. The fine print says you do what I tell you to do. Only what I tell you to do. Are we clear, pumpkin?"

"Whatever."

He moved in like an unwanted shadow, and he ran a strict program. He was also very systematic. Morning coffee. Evening security sweeps. Waiting by the door when I tried to leave. I couldn't step onto my own patio without him watching the fence line. It was like we were tied at the hip, and it got on my nerves.

"Do you ever relax?" I snapped one afternoon.

"When the threats stop," he uttered without looking up from his phone.

"What threats? All I see are flowers and sympathy cards."

"That's the point, Nuri. People don't send warnings when they're serious about fucking you up. It just happens."

"This is boring as hell," I said, crossing my arms. "Reid, I feel like I'm suffocating."

"Ha. You're suffocating, yet you're still breathing. You're welcome."

I hated how he always had the right answer for everything and how calm he was, how immovable and unshakeable he appeared. I only wished I had that kind of chill.

"You know I had a life before this," I whined. "I went to meetings. I had dinner with my girls. I went to events and hung out from time to time. You know, normal stuff."

"And now you have enemies," Reid countered. "A lot of them."

"What do you mean, a lot?"

"Yes. People Jahi dealt with. People who owe money. People who don't want their names coming up in the wrong conversations. People who may have been suspicious about what Jahi discovered."

I swallowed hard. "You think they'd kill me?"

"Of course I do. You do as well, because if you didn't think that, would I be here? You and I both know you aren't as clueless as you're pretending to be. You read that letter and saw those files. There are lots of people with a shit ton to lose. But don't sweat it. Just keep moving how I tell you to move, and you will be fine."

"How long do I have to live like this? I've got shit I want to do," I whined.

"You can't do anything if you're dead now, can you? Just sit tight. And to answer your question, until one of them gets bold enough to come for you. After they see what I do to his ass, the others will scatter."

Armani showed up a week later. This time, Reid answered the door. I heard Armani's voice before I saw him.

"Who the hell are you?"

"Reid. Her security," he replied flatly. "If you jump that gate again, you'll never jump another one."

"Watch out man," Armani said as he tried to shrug Reid off. "Where is Nuri?"

"She's not seeing anyone."

I stepped into the hallway just as my name was being mentioned.

His eyes flicked to Reid, then back to me. "So this is what we're doing now?"

"This is what I need." I shot back.

Armani stepped inside anyway, his gaze never leaving Reid. "You didn't even look at what I gave you, did you?"

"I did," I shrugged. "Then I threw that shit in the trash."

His jaw tightened. "Why would you do that, Nuri? That was stupid."

"No, that was me choosing not to be manipulated. Whatever Jahi had going on should have ended the second his ass went into the ground. I told you I didn't know shit, so leave me alone, please."

Armani huffed, and Reid shifted slightly. It was a warning, and Armani noticed.

"So you're her guard dog now?"

"Careful. I'm nobody's dog."

Armani smirked. "Sir, Reid, whatever your name is. You can chill out. Nuri trusts me," he said confidently as he started toward me.

Reid stepped in front of him, blocking his path to me.

"No, she doesn't, and it wouldn't matter if she did. I'm her security, and I don't trust men who orbit chaos, especially ones with feelings. You don't know me, but I know all about you."

Armani stepped closer to Reid, and Reid did the same. Eye to eye. Muscle to muscle.

I stepped between them. "Enough. You two can put your dicks away."

Armani's eyes softened when he looked at me. "You don't need him, Nuri."

"I do, because he's honest about what he is."

"And what's that?" Armani asked.

"A man who would kill for me without pretending it's love," I spat. Reid didn't deny it.

Armani flicked his nose. "I never lied to you about who I was. I was clear from the beginning. The funny thing is, you were okay with who I was until someone came along and told you not to be."

It felt like all the air was being sucked out of the room. Armani's eyes were locked on me, as if he were trying to tap into my soul. For a brief, terrifying moment, I thought Reid might actually draw his weapon.

"Reid," I said quietly.

He didn't look at me. "He shouldn't be here."

"He's leaving," I said.

Armani looked up at me, pleading with his eyes. "You think this makes you safe?"

"I think it makes me awake."

He nodded slowly. "Call me when you remember who you are." He shot Reid one last gaze and stormed toward the door.

"I never forgot who I was. And I haven't forgotten who you are either," I shouted as the door closed.

Reid locked it behind him, checked the cameras, then finally looked at me.

"He is trouble," he grumbled.

"I know."

"Why am I just now hearing about him coming over? Is he the reason why you hired me?"

"Yes. The last time he came over, he said somebody was coming for me. He gave me a photo with a name and number to the man I saw at the funeral. I threw it away. I was sick and tired of all this gangster shit. I'm no gangster. I'm just a girl who wants to live a regular life. I didn't even have an hour to be a normal widow. No time to grieve. Just time to worry, and I was sick of it. He tried to convince me I could trust him, but I could never. He lost my trust years ago, years before all this shit happened, and he would never get it back."

"Do you still have any of those things? The photograph, the name, or address? You need to make it clear to him to never return. He has no business here unless he's coming to confess some shit and pay you the money he owed your husband, which I'm sure he's said nothing about."

"No," I shook my head. "I don't have any of those things anymore, and you're right. He hasn't mentioned the specifics of his business dealings with Jahi."

"And he never will. Just know this. He's the type of man that won't stop sniffing around. His ego is too damn big."

"I know," I admitted.

Reid leaned against the counter, arms crossed. "Let me explain something to you. Something you may not be aware of."

"What, Reid?"

He drew in a sharp breath, "I don't argue, and I don't get loud. I get lethal."

I met his gaze. My heart was pounding, not with fear, but with clarity. For the first time since Jahi died, I was standing my ground, and everyone would feel it.

Chapter Eleven

By the time the girls came around again, my house felt different. Armani showing up unannounced and Reid answering the door instead of me had shifted the energy in a way I didn't quite know how to name yet. It wasn't attraction...at least that's what I told myself, but something about seeing another man step into my space so firmly, so calmly, without fanfare or explanation, cracked open a door I hadn't realized I'd closed.

Days after Armani left, Reid remained calm yet watchful.

Not hovering. Not pacing. Just...present. Sitting at my kitchen island, sipping water like a normal human being instead of the walking threat assessment he'd been for days. He even laughed once, even if it was quiet and under his breath.

When Paige texted me, *I hope you're ready to get your ass whooped because we are on the way,* I didn't tell him. I figured he'd find out.

They arrived loud, as expected. Paige burst through my front door like she paid a mortgage here. Charity was right behind her, carrying wine and opinions, and Maya brought baked goods, a charcuterie board, and her Bible. The noise alone made my chest loosen. My house had been holding its breath, and it finally exhaled.

Reid stood when they walked in. He was polite, respectful, and already clocking body language, exits, tone. Paige was clocking something else entirely.

"Oh," she muttered while staring at Reid. "So this is who you've been cooped up in the house with?"

Reid blinked.

Charity didn't even try to be subtle. "Wow. You did not tell us it was Mr. Fine Fine from the examiner's office. Shidd... I wish you had told me. I would have worn something sexier."

Maya closed her eyes immediately. "Jesus."

I rubbed my forehead while grabbing Paige's arm. "Please don't start this shit."

Paige ignored me, walking a slow circle around Reid like she was checking out a luxury vehicle. "He got that quiet kind of fine. Like he don't talk much, but when he does, everybody listens."

Reid blushed so hard I thought he would crack a cheekbone.

"Hello, ladies. I'm Reid. We haven't been formally introduced," he said, extending his hand.

Paige shook it enthusiastically. "Heyyyy, I'm Paige. I talk too much and mind everybody's business."

Charity smiled. "Hi. I'm Charity. I notice things."

Maya waved awkwardly. "I'm Maya, and I apologize in advance for these two." She pointed at Charity and Paige.

From there, the night went exactly where it shouldn't have. Spades turned competitive immediately. Paige and Charity accused each other of cheating within the first two hands. Maya tried to invoke Christian ethics into a card game that had none. And Reid somehow ended up sitting in the corner, pretending he was just there to make sure nobody died, while very obviously listening to everything.

At some point, Paige leaned over and whispered—but not whispering at all—"Why he keep looking at you like that?"

"I don't know what you're talking about," I said, putting my head down and focusing on my hand.

"He looks at you like you're the assignment."

"Girl, that's a good thing because I *am* the assignment. I pay him well to watch me."

Maya sighed. "Can we please not objectify the security?"

"I'm not objectifying," Paige waved her off. "I'm observing, and the wine is helping."

Eventually, the conversation shifted, as it always did, to questions nobody wanted to answer.

"So," Charity said casually, shuffling the deck like she wasn't setting a trap. "What was in the safe?"

I shot back, "Nothing major."

Paige's head snapped up. "See, that was a lie."

"It wasn't."

"It was," Paige insisted. "Your voice went up."

Charity nodded. "Girl, we've been knowing you for years. You are a terrible-ass liar."

Maya frowned. "Nuri..."

I shrugged. "Just jewelry. Diamonds. Random things."

Paige leaned back before yoking her neck forward. "Men don't hide diamonds in wall safes. They hide secrets or crimes. And women don't hire around the clock security unless some serious shit is going on."

Reid shifted slightly but stayed quiet.

"I'm not lying to you," I said, irritation creeping in. "I just don't want to talk about it."

Charity studied me for a long moment, then softened. "Okay."

Paige didn't. "I don't believe you."

"I don't need you to," I snapped.

Maya reached for my hand. "We just don't want you carrying everything alone."

"I'm fine, and I'm not alone, as you can see."

They didn't argue after that, which meant they understood.

Later, much later, when the wine and liquor were gone and truth flowed easier, Paige flopped back against the couch and slurred, "What do y'all even like in a man?"

Charity answered immediately. "Tall. Quiet. Emotionally unavailable but polite."

Maya groaned. "That's not healthy."

Paige smirked. "I like a man who looks like he could change a tire *and* my life."

I laughed so hard I snorted.

That's when Reid walked into the kitchen for water.

Silence.

Every single one of us froze.

Paige blinked. "Oh my God."

Charity covered her face. "I want to crawl into the fireplace."

"I told y'all. Y'all have no couth," Maya whispered. "Don't be ashamed now. Just keep on talking."

Reid paused, glass in hand, eyes flicking between us. "I was just...thirsty."

We laughed until tears streamed down our faces.

Then my phone rang. It was my mother. Of course she

would call on one of the only nights where I actually had joy in my heart. She launched straight into inappropriate territory with barely a breath in between—asking questions about Jahi, telling me what had gone awry at work because of his absence, saying I didn't care enough because I hadn't stepped foot into that building since he passed.

Paige snatched the phone before I could stop her.

"Ma'am," Paige said calmly, "this is not the time, place, or dimension. Go find you something else to do."

She hung up and handed the phone back like she'd done a civic duty.

The night ended in laughter—cards scattered, wine gone, my house loud and alive, and I loved it. And Reid was still quiet, still watching and assessing, but he no longer felt like just security.

He felt...present.

He felt like a friend and I was grateful.

Chapter Twelve

The loud mouths eventually surrendered to exhaustion and drunkenness. One by one, the girls faded out. Paige was stretched across the couch like she'd declared squatters' rights. Charity was curled up with a throw blanket, her phone still clutched in her hand. And Maya was tucked neatly into the guest room after insisting on a prayer session none of us was sober enough to participate in. Their laughter lingered even after they were knocked out. My heart held onto the warmth they'd brought with them, and I didn't want to let it go.

I stood in the hallway for a moment, listening. For the first time all night, everything was quiet. Reid hadn't moved much. He never did when things settled. He waited, like stillness was part of his job description. When our eyes met, there was an unspoken understanding between us that neither of us was ready for sleep yet.

"Want to sit somewhere else?" he asked quietly.

"Yes," I said eagerly. Too eagerly.

We ended up on the back patio. The air was cool and brisk. Atlanta hummed softly in the distance. It was the southern city that never fully slept. It just rested its eyes a little. Reid leaned against the railing with his hands tucked into his pockets. His posture was relaxed in a way I hadn't seen before. For the first time, he wasn't in protector mode. He was just present.

"I didn't always plan to do this, you know," he said after a moment.

"This...you mean protect widows from their own lives?"

A corner of his mouth lifted. "That too. I went to college thinking I had it all figured out. I majored in business, graduated, got the degree, then realized I hated every version of the life it was supposed to give me."

"What happened?"

He shrugged. "I'm still not sure. I just know I felt empty. Like I'd checked all the boxes and still missed the mark."

"So what did you do?"

He shrugged again. "I joined the Marine Corps. I figured if I didn't know what I wanted, I at least knew I wanted discipline and purpose. I wanted something that didn't feel fake."

I nodded slowly. "That makes sense."

He looked at me then. Really looked. "What about you?"

I hesitated, then let the truth come the way it had been pressing all night. "I didn't see my life going in this direction. I'm just like every girl in the world. I wanted to fall in love and stay there, but as you know, shit don't always go the way we plan. The last two years of my marriage were... performative, to say the least. The public appearances, the charity galas, smiling for cameras. It was all for show. I didn't feel like he loved me anymore, and he did nothing to change my mind."

"For months, Jahi stopped touching me, stopped looking at me like I was his. He stopped wanting me, and that fucked me up mentally for a while. At first, he did the most to get me. I wasn't studying him. I was still trying to move past the damage Armani caused. But Jahi wrapped that package of lies so well, I couldn't resist it. Like they used to say back in the day, I fell for the okey-doke."

Reid didn't interrupt.

"We used to be so passionate. We couldn't keep our hands off each other. But somewhere along the way, his job became his obsession. The deals. The power that came with it. The glamour. I never wanted that life the way he did."

I swallowed. "And maybe whatever he discovered... whatever was weighing on him...pulled him even further away."

Reid's voice was gentle. "That kind of stress changes people, Nuri."

"Or reveals them," I said softly.

He was quiet for a moment before speaking again. "I've been celibate for four years."

I turned to him with a raised brow, surprised at the admission.

"I made a promise. I told God I didn't want to move from loneliness into the wrong arms. I wanted to wait until I felt peace, not chemistry."

The honesty in his voice undid me more than anything else that night.

"And now?"

He met my eyes. "Now I'm trying not to confuse timing with intention."

The moment stretched as the air shifted.

I didn't remember who moved first, only that suddenly we were close enough to feel each other breathe. The kiss happened softly, almost accidentally, like something neither of us had planned but both had needed. It lasted only a second, but it radiated in my pussy long after.

Then the guilt rushed in, fast and loud. We pulled back at the same time.

"I shouldn't..." I started.

"I know," he said.

"I'm still—"

"I know," he repeated.

We stood there, hearts racing and eyes locked.

"I'll be in the guest room at the end of the hall if you need me."

"I'll...be upstairs in my bedroom," I replied.

We didn't speak any other words. There were no promises or lingering around. Just a shared understanding that something had shifted and that we weren't ready to touch it again yet.

We walked in separate directions through the quiet house, both wide awake, both carrying the weight of a kiss that felt like a beginning and a mistake all at once. Neither of us slept easily after that.

The house was still. Even the city outside felt muted, like Atlanta itself was taking a nap. I lay there listening.

Paige snored softly downstairs, dramatic even in sleep. Charity's laugh from earlier still echoed faintly in my ears. Maya was sleeping peacefully under God's watchful eye. But danger didn't announce itself. It never does. It arrived quietly, the way unease always had in my life.

I started to feel off while staring at the ceiling. My

body caught the wave before my mind caught up. Sliding out of bed quietly, I wrapped a robe around myself as I stepped out of my room. I didn't call out for Reid. I didn't have to. I looked up, and he was already there at the end of the hallway, shirt off, muscles contracting, and fully awake. He wasn't startled to see me, and he didn't seem surprised I was up.

"You feel it too?" I whispered.

He nodded once. "I've been feeling it for a while now."

My stomach tightened. "What's going on?"

"Someone's outside," he said calmly. "They're not trying to get in. They're just...watching."

A chill slid down my spine. "How do you know?"

"Because they are still there. They want to be seen. Come here. I'll show you."

I followed him to the security monitor in the study. The screens glowed softly in the dark, each angle showing a quiet version of my property. The trees were barely moving, the street beyond calm and normal.

Then Reid zoomed in.

"There," he pointed.

A figure was near the edge of the property line. They weren't hiding, but not moving either. The person stood where the camera could catch a shoulder, the shape of a body, the suggestion of a man who knew exactly where to position himself.

A lump formed in my throat.

"What in the hell is he doing? It doesn't look like he's trying to break in."

"You're right. He isn't," Reid agreed. "He's reminding you."

"Reminding me of what?"

"That you're not forgotten."

I wrapped my arms around myself, suddenly very aware of how vulnerable the house felt with my friends scattered throughout it, trusting me to keep them safe.

"Do I need to get them up? Do they need to leave?" I asked quietly.

"No. That's why he's out there. He knows you won't risk them."

"What do we do now?"

Reid's jaw tightened. "I let him know I see him too."

He cocked his gun and stepped outside before I could stop him. I watched through the monitor as he crossed the yard slowly, cautiously, stopping short of the property line. The man didn't move. He didn't flinch. They were two silhouettes facing each other in the dark, neither willing to be the first to move.

After a moment, the figure stepped back. Then vanished.

Reid came inside a minute later, locking the door behind him.

"He gone?" I asked.

"For now."

I exhaled shakily. "What the hell? They didn't have to do all that."

"They did," Reid said. "They wanted you unsettled."

"Well, congratulations to them. They sure as hell did that."

He looked at me, not with alarm or pity but with something steadier. "I told you not to worry. I won't let anything happen to you. I got you for real."

I believed him.

We stood there for a moment longer, the house settling again, danger retreating just enough to remind us it hadn't disappeared. When I finally went back to bed, I didn't sleep. I couldn't. Neither did Reid. And somewhere beyond the reach of my cameras, someone was already deciding what their next move would be.

The morning came softly. Sunlight crept through the curtains the color of warm amber, landing on the marble floor. I lay awake longer than necessary, staring at the ceiling, replaying the night in pieces that didn't line up neatly. The laughter. The cards. The way Reid had looked at me when the house finally settled. The way that kiss had happened without permission and ended just as quickly, like both of us were afraid of what would happen if we lingered.

I finally got up, moving slowly, careful not to wake anyone. Paige was now sprawled across the couch in a way that suggested she had fought sleep and lost spectacularly. Charity was still curled up on the loveseat, her and her lashes resting peacefully like nothing in the world was wrong. Maya's door was cracked just enough for me to hear her steady breathing, calm and unbothered, faith intact.

Scattered shoes, half-empty wineglasses, and shot glasses littered the table. Paige's purse sat flung open like it had been robbed in the night. The house smelled faintly of coffee grounds and something sweet Maya had baked, and for a few fragile seconds, it felt almost...normal.

Almost.

I padded into the kitchen. Reid was already there. He stood by the counter with his coffee mug in hand. He was dressed in yesterday's clothes, like sleep had never quite happened for him either. He looked quieter in the morning. Less guarded somehow. Human in a way that felt intimate without trying to be.

"Good morning," he said softly.

"Is it really that good?" I replied, reaching for a mug.

He smiled faintly. "Absolutely it is. You're alive, aren't you?"

We stood there for a moment in silence. This time, I was aware of how close we were, not physically, but emotionally. I got the feeling that something sacred was sitting between us, but it was still waiting to be unraveled.

"They didn't notice anything?" I asked.

"No. They slept through everything."

Relief washed over me, followed by gratitude and trust.

"Good," I murmured. "I guess it wasn't a bad thing that they got white-girl wasted last night."

Paige chose that moment to shuffle into the kitchen, hair wild, eyes squinting like the light had personally slapped her in the face.

"Why does my body feel like it lost a fight?" she groaned.

"You drank," Charity's voice floated in from the living room. "And talked too much last night, as usual. I'm surprised that isn't all that's hurt. Your tongue should be tired too."

"I regret nothing," Paige said, then froze when she noticed Reid. "Oh. Good morning, tall protector of peace."

Reid chuckled and cleared his throat. "Morning."

Leaning against the counter, Paige studied us both. "Why do y'all look like that?"

"Like what, Paige?" I muttered, rolling my eyes.

"I can't quite explain it. You look guilty. Like you two

did something that I would've done and enjoyed." She smirked and bit her lip.

"We did not."

Charity appeared behind her, her eyes sharp as usual. "You definitely did."

Maya entered last. "Did I miss anything?"

"No," Reid and I said in agreement. "Nothing."

Paige grinned. "That's a yes."

The rest of the morning unfolded calmly, too calm considering what had happened just hours before. Paige insisted on making breakfast, which turned into her supervising Charity while Maya prayed over the food. Reid stayed nearby but not hovering. He did his usual, watching the doors, the windows, the energy of the room without drawing attention to himself.

At one point, Paige leaned toward me and whispered, "He looks at you like he wanna crack that back."

I elbowed her. "Girl, stop. That man is working. He's not studying me."

"I will not," she whispered back. "I'm just calling it like I see it."

Later, when the girls started gathering their things, the mood shifted. Reality crept back in as hugs lingered a little longer than usual and promises to check in were repeated like oaths. When the front door finally closed behind them, the house inhaled again.

Reid and I stood in the quiet, but the absence was loud.

"I should do another sweep of the property," he muttered as he headed out the front door.

"Okay," I nodded.

When he finished, he returned to the kitchen, resting his hands on the counter across from me.

"About last night," he began.

I lifted my hand gently. "We don't have to name it or even talk about it. I'm good if you are."

He studied me for a moment, then nodded. "Fair."

"But," I added softly, "thank you again for taking this on...me on, and for being here."

"You don't have to thank me. It has been my pleasure. You're a good girl, Nuri. You deserve the best life has to offer, and you deserve a life free from fear, free from wondering, and definitely free from suffering from someone else's mistakes."

His words made me feel like I wasn't alone in this thing anymore. Not alone in the house. Not alone in the fear or in the long, uncertain road ahead.

Whatever danger waited for me outside these walls needed to get comfortable with the fact that I was no longer standing by myself.

I had a mean, thorough, unwavering, fine-ass sidekick.

Chapter Thirteen

The threat didn't come with noise. It didn't shatter glass or kick doors in like one would have expected. Instead, it arrived the way bad things usually do in life...quietly, suddenly, and patiently waiting to be noticed.

I was standing at the kitchen sink, peering out the window when I saw it. At first, my brain refused to register what my eyes were clearly seeing. Muscle memory took over instead. Rinse the mug. Dry your hands. Set it down. It wasn't until I turned back toward the window that something pulled at my attention. A wrongness I couldn't quite put my finger on.

My car was parked in the driveway where I'd left it. It looked the same, but something was different. I leaned closer to the window.

As I stared, I realized the car was fine, but my rose bush that the car was parked beside was not. Every other rose on my iceberg bush was gone. My breath hitched, not sharply or dramatically, but in the subtle way the body reacts before the mind has time to catch up. I stood there too long, staring, trying to convince myself I was being paranoid, but I knew I wasn't.

I didn't call out to Reid, nor did I move an inch. I just waited.

Reid appeared beside me a moment later, close enough that I felt his presence before I saw it.

"You see it too," he said quietly.

I nodded. "Someone was here. That rose bush was the only thing I contributed to this home. Literally the only thing. I insisted on having white roses in the yard. So much that I did it myself. I'm so pissed."

Reid checked the cameras again from his phone. This time, he didn't rush outside or grab his weapon. He stood still, just like me. His eyes scanned the yard, the street, and the tree line beyond the fence like he was reading a language I didn't know how to speak.

"Someone came to my house, cut my shit, and left. This is getting weird."

"Yes, they did."

"Why would they do such childish things?" I asked.

Reid turned to me then. "Because they wanted you to

notice. They didn't want you to panic or call the police. Just notice. They are fucking with you."

I wrapped my arms around myself. "They could have done more."

"Of course they could, but they chose not to," he said. "And that's the message."

I swallowed hard. "Which is?"

I can reach you.

Reid didn't say it out loud, but I could tell that's what he meant from the look on his face. He stepped outside carefully, checking the driveway, the tires, the gas tank, the underside of the car. I watched from the doorway, every nerve sparked. My house suddenly felt too open and too exposed. In that very moment, I wished I could have cloned him and made twenty Reids to protect me.

When he came back in, his face was calm, but I'd learned enough by now to know what that meant.

"No damage," he said. "No tracker, and no one appears to have tampered with anything."

"That you can see," I chirped.

"That I can see."

I exhaled slowly. "So what now?"

"Now we document it, and we don't change your routine."

I laughed once in disbelief. "Someone came to my home and touched my property."

"And if you up and leave or disappear," he said gently, "they know they got to you."

I shook my head in agreement, even though every instinct in my body screamed otherwise.

He met my eyes. "You're doing good, Nuri. Everything will be fine."

That care in his voice provided immediate comfort.

Later that afternoon, after Reid finished another sweep and the house settled again, I went outside alone for the first time that day. I stood beside my car, staring at the rose bush. None of the roses that were cut were on the ground. They were gone. I wondered if someone took them as some kind of sick memento. The thought made my skin crawl.

I stood there seething. As I began to walk away, that's when I saw it. A small white card tucked under my windshield wiper. I froze.

"Don't touch it," Reid yelled. I hadn't noticed he was standing behind me. He reached into his pocket and pulled out a napkin. Pulling the card free, he turned it over carefully.

There was nothing written on it. No threats, warnings, or names. Just a plain card.

Anger coursed through my veins. "They are really fucking with me, and it's pissing me off, Reid. There's nothing on the card?"

Reid's jaw flexed. "It's by design, Nuri. They know you'll imagine worse than anything they could've written. This is a mind fuck. Don't let it shake you. You've come a long way. Don't step back now."

"Oh, I won't," I said as I looked back at my house. My quiet street. The place I'd always felt untouchable.

"You came out here earlier and saw nothing out of place. That means they came back. They came here twice," I groaned.

"Yes."

"And that means most likely they'll come back."

"Yes, they will." Reid folded the card and slipped it into an evidence bag. "But not today," he added. "Today, they just wanted you thinking about them."

I shook my head slowly, fear settling into something colder, steadier. Because whoever was watching me wasn't reckless. They were patient. And that meant this wasn't over. Not even close.

I sauntered back into the house, determined not to let what just happened get to me. I'd fired all the help the second my husband parted from his earthly life, and there was now lots to do in this house besides live in it. Every nook and cranny had to be swept, mopped, and dusted. Reid kept a watchful eye and offered to help, but I declined. This was something I needed and wanted to do. A welcome distraction from my reality.

I got a little too heavy-handed with bleach, and because of it, both of us were forced outside from the fumes.

The moment I got the back door open, Reid turned to me.

"Listen, I know many women clean as a stress reliever, and trust me, I want you to do your thing. I'm just not trying to die in the process," Reid said as we sat out back on the patio.

"I know. I'm so sorry," I chuckled. "I don't know what in the hell I was thinking. If I'd mixed another concoction, they wouldn't have to come finish me off. I would have done it myself...involuntarily, of course."

We both laughed.

"I saw you pouring bottle after bottle of cleaning solution into the bleach water. I just knew I was going to find your ass stretched out on the bathroom floor. I thought to myself...she's trying to kill us. Hell, the bleach was enough by itself," he grinned.

"In my defense, we always had maids and cleaners growing up. I didn't have to clean, cook, or do anything domestic when I was a child. Nothing but sit back, be quiet, and be the perfect little Southern belle."

"Something about the way you said that makes me think you preferred to be something else," Reid said as he stared into my eyes.

"You're right. I wanted to be myself. Just...Nuri. Unfortunately, that wasn't good enough for my mother. Everything about me and my life was perfectly curated. The way I walked, talked, sat down, stood up. My posture. The way I ate my food. Literally everything. That's the reason I went in my own direction the minute I graduated high school. I couldn't wait to get away from the invisible shackles."

"How did you avoid getting wrapped up in the family business?" he asked.

"Easy. I simply refused. I went to a community college and majored in something that had nothing to do with business. I went to school for HVAC."

Reid side-eyed me for a moment, then cracked up laughing. "You've got to be kidding me. You mean to tell me you know how to install an air conditioner?"

"Yep, and run pipes through the ceiling. I did installs, repairs, wiring, and everything. I did it all."

"Well, I'll be damn," he grinned. "I would have never guessed that in a million years. Girl, you are full of surprises, aren't you?"

"I guess I am," I smirked.

"Were they upset?"

"Of course. My mother was furious. My father was supportive. He didn't care. He just wanted his baby happy. My mother wanted me to attend a four-year college and major in business, but I was grown, and they couldn't force me to do anything anymore. Every six months or so, she would try to pitch me some new bullshit or rave about a portion of the company they were creating specifically for me. Something I could run all on my own. At least that's what she would tell me. And every time, I politely declined. I wanted nothing to do with the consortium.

"Just when I was getting through to her that they would never be able to get me involved with the family business, I turned around and married a man who should have been my parents' son."

"Sounds like a dream come true," Reid said. "For them."

"It was. He fit right in with them. They saw the way he worked the room and the smile on his face when all eyes were on him. It was a done deal after that. They snatched him up, and he didn't look back. He didn't even put up a fight. He basically ran toward them despite seeing me run in the other direction. But that was Jahi. No one could tell him shit. Once he saw how they were living, the parties, the show, the money...he dove headfirst into the lifestyle."

"Enough about my parents," I said timidly. "Reid...I wanted to run something by you. First, just know I'm not asking your permission."

He gave me a peculiar look but perched up, readying himself for the bullshit.

"So, while I was cleaning and throwing out junk mail, I came across an invitation to a Black-tie charity gala on Friday at the Fox Theatre. Old money, familiar faces, and cameras guaranteed. It's the kind of event Jahi and I used to attend without thinking twice. We would sit there smiling and cheesing like our lives weren't quietly unraveling behind closed doors."

I stared at the ceiling, reminiscing, then reeled myself back in.

"I want to attend. Before you say anything, let me say this. You said it yourself not to run, or they would know they got to me. What better way than to pop out and show them how good I am?"

He stared at me before finally speaking. "What do you want me to say? You told me you weren't asking my permission, so what am I to do with this information?"

"You are supposed to say, 'I support your decision, and I'd be happy to accompany you and watch your back.'"

"I told you I wasn't a yes man. I wasn't one for your husband, and I won't be one for you. However, I'm not your father, and you are paying me to do a job. Which is to protect you. Even if I'm protecting you from yourself. So yes, I will come with you. If we do this, we must do this thing right. No half-stepping. Are we on the same accord?"

"We are. Thank you," I muttered as we fist-bumped.

"You know you don't have to prove anything, Nuri."

"I know," I replied. "I'm refusing to let them little-girl me."

He nodded once. "Okay then. Let's do this."

We did.

I stepped out of the house dressed in black silk that moved when I did. My hair was laid. Makeup flawless. Nails and feet brand new. As I held my head high, I felt something settle into place. Not confidence exactly, but resolve. I was tired of being managed by fear.

Stepping out of the SUV, the cameras caught me immediately.

"Nuri Laurent," someone called. "How are you holding up?"

I smiled softly. "I'm good. I'm taking things one day at a time."

Inside, the room buzzed with that familiar Atlanta energy. Power disguised as philanthropy and gossip dressed up as concern. I could feel the eyes on me. Some curious. Some empathetic. Others simply hating.

Good. Let them hate.

Reid stayed close without hovering. A quiet presence just over my shoulder. Not possessive, but protective. And because of him, I knew the difference.

I made the rounds. Accepted condolences. Donated generously while laughing at the right moments. I spoke

Jahi's name without flinching. Looking over my left shoulder, I saw my mother at the bar doing what she did best, flirting and drinking. I looked around for my father, but he was nowhere to be found. I figured she left him at home alone as usual. I considered walking over, then decided against it. If I had, she would have fucked up my night.

Then I felt it. The shift in the air.

Someone had their eyes on me.

I didn't see him at first, but I felt him. When I finally laid eyes on him, he didn't look away. He simply watched.

I lifted my glass slightly in his direction. It wasn't a toast. It was an acknowledgment.

Reid noticed immediately. "You see someone?"

"Yes."

"Do you want to leave?"

I shook my head. "Not yet."

The watcher lingered another minute, then slipped away into the crowd. No scene. No drama. Just recalibration.

Later, as the night wound down and the cameras moved on, Reid leaned in slightly. "Well, that was a bold move."

"So was coming to my house and cutting my fucking rose bush," I said.

He studied my face. "You're not afraid?"

"I am," I admitted. "I'm just not bowing down."

A flicker of pride crossed his face before he masked it.

When we finally stepped outside, the night air cool against my skin, I exhaled a breath I hadn't realized I'd been holding.

"They wanted me to retreat. To grieve quietly. To remain hidden and silent."

"And instead?" Reid asked.

"I showed up looking and feeling amazing."

He opened the car door for me. "You know they'll respond, right?"

"I know," I said, meeting his gaze. "But now they have to do it knowing I won't fold."

As we drove away, downtown lights flashing in the rearview mirror, I felt something solid beneath the fear.

I didn't know who had killed my husband yet, nor how far this shit would go, but I knew this much.

I was done shrinking.

And whoever thought intimidation would work on me had just learned their first lesson.

Chapter Fourteen

They didn't like that I smiled. That much became clear the next morning.

It wasn't dramatic. There were no broken windows, no alarms screaming, no masked men in the dark. Whatever line I'd crossed at the gala, they responded the way people that thought they had the upper hand always do. By reminding me that confidence was a privilege that could be easily revoked.

I realized something was wrong before Reid brought it to my attention. He'd been quiet too long. Normally, he moved through the house like rhythm, checking doors, windows, cameras with practiced efficiency. That morning, the silence stretched, thick and deliberate.

Walking into the study, I found him standing in front of the security monitor, jaw tight and eyes narrowed.

"What are you looking at, Reid?"

He didn't answer right away. Instead, he rewound the footage.

"There," he said, pointing at the monitor.

At first, I didn't see it. The driveway looked the same as it always did. Empty. Still and crafted in a way that once made me feel untouchable. Then the timestamp jumped back thirty minutes.

A car rolled slowly into frame. It was the same sedan that followed me home the night before Jahi died. It stopped just short of my gate. The driver didn't get out. They didn't need to. The window rolled down and a hand emerged and waved.

It wasn't hurried or threatening. It was casual and seemed familiar.

"They wanted you to know they saw you last night," Reid said quietly. "And they see you now."

I swallowed. "They didn't leave anything this time."

"That's the point," he replied. "They don't need to anymore."

I watched the footage again. The car didn't linger. They didn't circle around or hesitate. It simply pulled away, disappearing down the street like it had every right to be there.

"They are not trying to scare you; they are correcting you," Reid mumbled.

Those words settled deep. Correcting. As if my composure at the gala had been some kind of mistake or dig. As if my visibility disrupted a narrative they preferred intact.

I folded my arms tightly. "So, what's next because I'm really getting sick of this shit. They can fuck with me. Stalk my house. Leave shit on my window but they want to correct me. They have some damn audacity."

Reid met my eyes. "Now they push closer."

As if summoned by Reid's thoughts, my phone buzzed. It was an unknown number. Reid's posture shifted instantly. "Don't answer it."

The phone buzzed again then stopped. A second later, a notification appeared. Voicemail received.

I held my breath as I pressed play. There was no voice. Just sound. Noises like traffic, inaudible conversation, and the low hum of an alive city outside my walls. Then I heard something familiar. My laugh, then Jahi uttering a single phrase.

Crybaby

Which was something him and I joked about frequently. My first thought was to freak out. How could that be possible? I saw him. In the flesh. Dead and lowered in the ground yet I hear his voice clear as day, but then common sense kicked in. This had to mean the recording was old. Not current and the thought of someone recording him made me nauseous. Who would do such a thing? I wasn't sure but I had the feeling I would know soon enough.

"What did they say?"

"Nothing," my words came out faint. "They didn't say anything. What I heard was Jahi."

Reid's brow furrowed. "Are you sure it was your husband's voice?"

"I am. I'm not trying to be funny, but I think I know my own husband when I hear him."

"I didn't mean it like that, Nuri. I'm sorry. I was just saying, if you heard Jahi's voice, this means the recording is from the past. That proves someone has been watching you for much longer than we thought."

The weight of his words rattled my spirit. I sank into the chair. Suddenly exhausted.

"It's crazy they would do all this because I wasn't scared enough. Because I didn't behave the way they wanted. Hell, I'm not apologizing for surviving."

"You shouldn't have to," he said. "But you need to understand something."

I looked at him.

"They will escalate when they feel ignored," Reid continued. "Not because they want chaos but because they want control."

I exhaled slowly, fear shaping into something deeper. "Then they picked the wrong woman."

Outside, the street remained quiet. Ordinary. Impeccably calm. But I knew better now. Whoever was watching me wasn't watching to intimidate me anymore. They were watching to see how far they needed to go.

Then, the next week, without warning, Detective Dollars paid me another visit. I was in the living room pretending to read when Reid's posture changed near the front of the window. He didn't say anything but I'd learn to read his body language by now. He didn't reach for anything. Just shifted his weight and his eyes narrowed.

"Company," he said.

I looked up just as Detective Dollars stepped into view on the camera, standing on my porch like he belonged there.

Reid opened the door before I could say a word.

"Nuri," Dollars said, nodding at me as he stepped inside. "You look...steadier than last time."

"I had food," I replied. "It helped."

The corner of his mouth curled upward. "I see."

He didn't sit right away. He walked the room instead, eye taking in all the changes that were made since he last visited. The extra cameras, Reid's presence, the subtle tightening of everything. I introduced them to each other.

"Reid, this is Detective Dollars and Detective Dollars this is Reid, my protector and security. Whatever you need to say to me, you can say in front of him."

"You were seen last night," Dollars said finally.

"And."

"And you didn't flinch."

"Was I supposed to? I mean damn. I'm trying to move forward with my life. What does everyone want from me."

Dollars stopped pacing. Looked at me fully now. "That's why I'm here."

I folded my arms. "Then say it."

"I am positive you know by now someone's been watching you." He reached into his jacket and pulled out a slim folder. "There's a name tied to this man," he said. "Not the man himself...the one who hired him."

"Oh yeah, and how did you figure this out?"

"Well, that's on a need to know basis and you don't need to know. But just know, the department has eyes and ears everywhere. The how is not important. The who is."

Detective Dollars slipped a single photo onto the table. A man in his late forties, impeccably dressed. Familiar in the way powerful people always are. Someone you'd seen at galas, fundraisers and maybe even church. The kind of face Atlanta trusted without thinking twice.

I bucked my eyes. "I know him," I said quietly.

"Yes," Dollars replied. "You do."

The name followed.

Mercury Pointer

The air shifted. "That's not possible," I said. "He's –"

"A donor," Dollars finished. "A builder. A man who smiles for cameras and writes checks with commas."

"And he owed Jahi money. I've heard him mention his name a time or two," Reid said flatly.

Dollars nodded. "A lot. Enough to ruin him if it came out. Plus, we also learned Mercury had dealings with your husband at his job, but also this little criminal organization he had going on."

"Whatever you say Detective. I didn't know anything about that but what you're telling me is he's the one thats been sending someone to '*scare*' me?"

"Not at first," Dollars said. "At first, he waited. He wanted to see if grief would do the job for him. Make you retreat."

"And when it didn't?"

"He escalated," Dollars replied. "Subtly.

I laughed, once, loud and hollow. "Because I went to a damn gala."

"Because you reminded him you exist," Dollars said. "And worse...you reminded him you're composed, together and seemed to be thriving.."

Reid's voice was low. "I believe he's capable of more."

Dollars didn't deny. "Of course he is. They always are."

My chest tightened. "Then why hasn't he gone ahead and done what he really wants to do?"

"Because you're now visible," Dollars interrupted. "Right now, you're safer being seen than silenced. But that window doesn't stay open forever."

I stared at the photo again, Mercury Pointer. A man I'd hugged at parties. Smiled at and thanked for donations.

"A man like that doesn't get his hands dirty," I said.

"No," Dollars agreed. "He hires patience."

Finally, I looked up. "What do I do?

Dollars met my gaze. "You keep doing exactly what you're doing. You don't isolate. You don't act erratic. And you don't go to him. You let him come to you."

Reid nodded. "And I stay close."

"Yes," Dollars said. "Because he's not watching you to frighten you anymore."

"Then why?" I asked.

Dollars' voice dropped. "To decide if you're really a threat or just a minor inconvenience."

His statement and visit gave me clarity. Because now the watcher or the person behind him had a face and a name and it wasn't the one Armani had given me. It made me wonder if he purposely tried to divert my attention elsewhere or if he truly was trying to warn me. It didn't matter because I didn't put anything past anyone. Jahi said I couldn't trust anyone and if I didn't listen to him when he was alive, I sure as hell was listening now.

Detective Dollars gathered his things and headed for the door. "I'll be in touch. This part requires patience."

Chapter Fifteen

After he left, Reid turned to me. "You okay?"

"No," I said honestly as I looked at the photo one last time before sliding it back into the folder. "But at least now I know who I'm dealing with."

Reid nodded. "That changes things."

"It definitely does because fear without a face is paralyzing, but fear with a name can be handled.

A couple days after Detective Dollars left, I received another batch of flowers. They arrived late morning, when the house was still and the street looked harmless. Things had been eerily quiet, and I knew it wouldn't be long before someone made some noise. This seemed to be the new pattern.

A white town car pulled up at the gate. Reid asked if I

was familiar with the vehicle. I wasn't. He buzzed them through, thinking it was a family member coming by to show their respects. Reid was already at the door before the bell finished ringing.

I watched from the hallway. The delivery man didn't hesitate. He handed over an arrangement so large it required both arms, all white blooms...orchids, calla lilies, roses cut so perfectly they looked artificial. It was tasteful, impeccable, and alarming because once I was able to get past the beauty, I realized they were funeral flowers.

My stomach dropped.

"There's a card," Reid said once the door closed.

Of course there was. He didn't hand it to me right away. He read it first, eyes scanning quickly, jaw tightening before he passed it over.

The handwriting was elegant.

Nuri,

It's evidently clear Atlanta missed you the other night. I'm glad you're finding your footing in this big cold world alone. Grace under pressure is a rare thing.

Best regards, M.P.

I wasn't sure what to think of this. He didn't issue any threats, no demands, no name spelled out.

I let out a slow breath. "He knows exactly how this looks."

"Yes," Reid replied. "That's why he did it."

I stared at the flowers. "I can't believe this muthafucka sent me a damn funeral arrangement."

Reid's voice was quiet. "For you, as a reminder."

I laughed softly. "This was underwhelmingly creative."

The flowers sat on my table like a performance piece. Beautifully wrong but loud in their silence. Then my phone rang. Unknown number.

Reid shook his head once. "Let me."

"No," I said. "I want to hear him."

I answered.

"Nuri," Mercury's voice said smoothly, like we were best friends. "I hope I'm not interrupting."

"You're not," I replied evenly.

"I wanted to personally extend my condolences again," he continued. "Your husband was...complicated. But loss has a way of clarifying what matters."

I pictured him with a shit-eating grin as he spoke.

"I received your flowers." I spat.

"I hoped you would. Atlanta can be so cold when it wants to be. I thought a reminder of beauty might help."

"Help what? They're funeral flowers," I muttered.

A pause, then a soft chuckle. "Only if you are choosing to see them that way."

There it was. That hidden razor in the expensive chocolate.

"I see them for what they fucking are. Funeral flowers. This shit isn't funny at all. You think you're so cute, don't you?"

"Nuri, I wanted to tell you how I admired how composed you were at the gala," he went on. "Strength looks good on you. Just remember, visibility has a way of inviting opinions."

"I'm going to tell you like I told my mother. I don't give a damn about people's opinions of me. I could give a fuck less."

"Well now, Nuri. Who knew a woman with such grace and elegance had such a potty mouth. It's a welcomed surprised."

"Fuck you," I barked. "How's that for a damn potty mouth."

Another pause.

"Be well, Nuri."

The line went dead.

I stood there for a long moment, phone still pressed to my ear. My heart was steady in a way that surprised me.

"Guess I don't have to ask if that was him?" Reid stated.

"Yes, that was his smug ass. Just like you and Dollars said, he wants me unsettled. He mentioned how composed I was at the gala."

I sat the phone down and walked to the table, staring at the flowers one last time before making a decision that felt like instinct.

"Throw these fuckers out, "I demanded. "Get rid of them."

Reid didn't question it. He carried them outside and immediately dropped them into the trash bin. As the lid closed, something inside me hardened. It wasn't fear or anger. It was resolve.

"He thinks politeness makes him untouchable," I quipped.

Reid looked into my eyes. "Men like him rely on that."

"Then he just told me exactly how he wants to be fought," I replied. "Intimidation wrapped in courtesy is still intimidation, and I don't fuck with that."

Mercury made the mistake of thinking his flowers would shake me. They didn't. I was just paying closer attention now.

The house didn't calm down after Mercury's call.

If anything, it felt like the walls had absorbed it all...the audacity, the threat wrapped in courtesy, and now everything echoed differently. I tried to busy myself, moving from room to room without purpose, rearranging things, reading, scrolling TikTok. Anything to remind myself I was still here, still solid, still breathing. But my body refused to settle. My nerves stayed awake, buzzing and on edge, and on top of it all, anger was the emotion I felt most.

Reid saw it before I admitted it.

"You're not okay," he said quietly from behind me.

I didn't turn around. "I'm pissed, but I will be fine."

Walking over to me, he lifted my chin. "How about I cook us a nice dinner. We can sit, relax, and reflect. If you don't want to reflect, we can sit in silence. It's your game tonight, and you make the rules."

"Wait...you know how to cook? Why didn't I know this?"

"Nuri, you can fill a book with the things you don't know about me. I can burn with the best of them. Before you ask, nobody taught me. I taught myself. Before Instagram, Facebook, and TikTok, there was the Food Network. My mother watched that shit day and night. She didn't cook really, but she loved watching. Since we only had one TV, I watched with her and took an interest. I also love to bake. I make a mean pineapple upside-down cake." He smiled as he headed towards the kitchen.

"Of all the shit I've heard today, this pleases and surprises me the most. I would have never guessed that you loved to cook?"

"Not to brag, but do you see this body? This body was made in the kitchen. I cook all my own meals and rarely eat out. I prefer to know exactly what is going into my food. Anyway, I'm going to get started."

He opened the pantry and began searching for something to put together. I was low key ashamed because I cooked, but not cooked-cooked. If he was a fitness rat the way he claimed to be, nothing in my pantry would interest him, and I was right because seconds later he closed the pantry and turned to me.

"I'm going to place a delivery order for some real food because all you've got in here is processed junk. I'm not feeding you this."

I smiled and pulled up a chair as he scrolled the Publix website. When he was done, he came and took a seat next to me.

"Nuri, tell me something. What do you see your life like after all this bullshit comes to an end? Like, what will you do? What are your interests?"

I sucked in a deep breath. "I had so many ideas for my future, but as of right now, I can't think beyond this. I mean, who wakes up one day and is thrust into a world of secrets, crime, and stalking? This is unfathomable in so many ways to most people, me being one of them. The only answer I can comfortably give you is I'm taking things one day at a time."

"I see."

I could tell he wanted to say more but was holding back.

"Why? Why would you ask me something like that, Reid?"

"Because I know you're going through a lot, but I want to be sure this situation doesn't ruin you. Deception from a loved one can actually change the way your mind works. All of our experiences do, but trauma like this can take people out. I don't want that to be your future, so promise me one thing."

"What's that?" I asked.

"Promise me that if things get too heavy for you, you'll seek help. Even after all this is over, grief can linger for years. I don't want you to sit in it. I want to know if you see you can't get past it, that you will reach out to someone you trust."

"That list is super short, Reid. You should know this already."

"I do. You know what I mean. Don't stay closed in. Get a therapist, talk to your girls, talk to me. Whatever makes you feel better. Okay?"

He grazed my cheek and swept my hair behind my ear. It was a tiny gesture, but it didn't go unnoticed.

"Okay. I promise."

I changed the subject. I didn't want things getting too

deep. "So, tell me. What's on the menu for tonight? What are you feeding me?"

A glimmer of happiness spread across his face as he answered.

"Let's see... I ordered lamb chops, golden Yukon potatoes, heavy cream, brown sugar, asparagus, some lemons, and a few other things. I'll let you figure it out from there. Oh, and for dessert, I'm making sweet tahini and date truffles," he gloated.

"I'm down with all that. That shit sounds delicious and I can't wait. I'm going to go upstairs and get ready. I'll be back down in a few, okay?"

"Take your time. I'll be right here." He flashed a smile.

Chapter Sixteen

I ran up the winding staircase grinning from ear to ear. I knew this wasn't a date, but Reid was good company when he wasn't breathing down my neck. I was excited at the thought of Reid thinking enough of me to want to see me smile. Good food always did that. I ran myself a hot bath and quickly submerged my body. The closeness I felt with Reid had my pussy thumping like a rabbit. I wanted to be touched, fucked, pleased, and teased. All the things I'd been starved of in my marriage.

I was trying so badly not to take it there with him, but he was irresistible. Everything about him turned me on, and I couldn't deny it. Not to myself anyway. I was doing a good job keeping my wants and needs at bay to everyone else. At least I hoped I was but it had been three months since Jahi passed. I was now hornier than a man that just finished a ten year jail sentence. As I soaked in the tub, my fingers began roaming. Trying to find something to please. I grabbed my breast and licked my nipples gently as I dove into my yoni with my other hand. Nothing felt like the real thing, but this would have to do for now.

I circled my clit with precision and pressure, then slid down to my center. Sliding one, then two fingers in. My back arched as the sensation rose. I slid my fingers in and out until I gave in to the tingle. It felt so damn good. I muffled my moans when what I wanted to do was scream out to the world. The orgasm hit so heavy, a single tear fell from my eye.

I finished bathing, dried off, and entered my closet in search of something comfortable to wear. This wasn't a date, so I needed to keep it simple. I found a cute little romper. I slid it on as I stared at Jahi's clothes. An unexplainable feeling washed over me. A feeling I couldn't quite put my finger on. I couldn't tell if I was missing him or loathing him. I shrugged it off and closed the closet door, sprayed a few sprays of my favorite perfume, and threw my tresses in a messy bun. Then I descended back down the stairs to find Reid whipping it up. He was definitely in his element. He hadn't noticed I was in the room. Classical music played over the speakers as he flipped, tossed, mixed, and sprinkled his way around the kitchen. I sat back and watched a while before stepping into his view.

"Well damn, Wolfgang...you've got it going on in here. This is a side of you I've never seen. You're always so damn serious, so intentional. It's great to see you in this light."

"Stop talking about it before I get embarrassed and shut down this whole kitchen operation. Then we'll both be starving and I'll feed you Ramen noodles." He chuckled.

I threw my hands up and backed away. I grabbed a barstool, sat down, and watched as he created a spread fit for a queen. He turned the stove off and reached for the expensive China, the ones I'd never used.

"Hold on, partner," I muttered. "I've got paper plates. I know you just slaved over a hot stove, but I don't plan on doing any dishes tonight."

"Do you think I can plate this masterpiece I've created on paper plates? I can't. Just sit back, Nuri, and let me do my thing. I've got this. Besides, there is a dishwasher."

Doing what I was told, I sat back and watched as he meticulously spooned the cream potatoes, followed by the beautifully glazed lamb chops onto the plate. Lastly, he placed the perfectly cooked asparagus beside the chops and walked them over to the dinner table.

"Come on over here and grub. I know you've got to be hungry."

He sauntered back into the kitchen for silverware and

poured us a glass of 2017 Château Mouton Rothschild cabernet.

"Reid, did that bottle come from the cellar? Because I'd never seen it in there before. This bottle goes for about $700.00. I know my cheap ass didn't buy it, and I don't recall Jahi purchasing it either."

He chuckled. "Calm down. Neither of you paid for it. It's one of my favorites. I knew at some moment I would get into this kitchen and burn. These gourmet ranges were calling my name. I had the wine delivered a few weeks ago. I hope you don't mind."

"Not at all," I responded while I bit into the perfectly cooked lamb.

Our dinner was filled with laughter, tears—some from joy, some from pain—reflections, predictions, and a lingering want on my end to be next to him. After we were done, I gathered our plates and headed into the kitchen to wash dishes.

"I thought you said you weren't doing dishes," he stated as he trekked into my space.

"I wasn't, but it was so damn good I started feeling guilty about you having to do both."

He grinned as he walked back to the table to grab his wine glass before perching up on a barstool. It was his turn to watch me be domestic. As I slid the last skillet into the water, my phone buzzed on the counter.

"Would you see who that is for me? My hands are wet."

Grabbing the phone, his brow furrowed as he read the name across the screen.

MOMMY DEAREST

"Well damn, is she that bad?" he giggled as he turned the phone around so I could get a glimpse.

"You may as well put that phone back on the countertop. I'm still not ready to speak to her. Especially after the shit she said to me the morning I called and told her Jahi was dead. And yes, she is absolutely a Mommy Dearest. If not her, she's the old bitch from Flowers in the Attic. I don't know which one was worse."

Reid looked like he wanted to know more but didn't ask. Which was best because that would have soured my whole mood.

"Now that you are bathed and fed. I guess there's nothing left for you to do but hit the sheets. You've had a long day. You should get some rest."

He stepped closer, slow and intentional, until I felt him there. The heat from his body, the steadiness, made my pulse jump. He didn't reach for me right away. He waited.

A lump settled in my throat.

I turned then, and whatever I'd been holding collapsed straight into him. My forehead pressed against his chest first, then my face, my breath uneven as his arms came around me like they'd been waiting. Not rushed. Not greedy. Just firm enough to let my body melt into to his. His arms felt like pure heaven.

I inhaled him...soap, clean cotton, and something warm and spicy. My body responded before my heart could caution it. My hands twisted lightly in his shirt, needing proof he was real. That he was close. My pussy got the message and began to grow slick. I wanted him so badly, I could taste it. I needed him to take me away from this mentally. To slide the bulge that was increasingly growing between us into my yoni and make me forget. If only for a moment.

"I'm exhausted," I whispered.

His hand slid slowly up my back, palm warm, grounding. "I know."

I pulled back just enough to look at him. His eyes were darker now. His pupils were dilated, and his jaw tight like he was holding himself in check by sheer will.

Unfortunately for me, sheer will was something I didn't possess. His touch had me wide open, and all my inhibitions were gone. Fuck doing the right thing. I wanted to do what felt right, and straddling him was all that came to mind.

"I don't want to be alone tonight. I'm tired of being alone," I said.

Something flickered across his face. Want mixed with restraint mixed with conflict. All of it passing too fast to name.

He kissed me softly at first. His mouth was warm, unhurried, fitting against mine with a precision that startled me. It wasn't rushed. It was deep, sweet, but passionate. It was what I needed.

My body leaned into his before my mind could intervene.

His hands came to my waist, thumbs pressing into the curve of my hips, steadying me as my knees weakened. I felt it everywhere. My nipples were rock hard against his chest. They were aching to be touched. His chest expanded with each breath, and the subtle flex of his arms turned me into puddy. Our tongues danced beautifully as we savored every second.

The kisses matured. Harder, deeper, needier. My body started remembering what it felt like to be wanted without being taken for granted. My fingers slid up his neck, into his hair, tugging just enough to draw a low sound from his chest that sent heat straight through me.

"Fuck," I moaned. "I want you in me so bad."

"And trust me, it's no place I'd rather be, Nuri."

My name on his lips opened the floodgate. My pussy creamed.

He kissed me again, slower this time. Then he stopped.

Not abruptly. Not coldly. Just stopped. He rested his forehead against mine, breath uneven, hands still firm at my waist like letting go would be worse.

"I can't go further," he said quietly. "I want to, but I can't."

Disappointment glinted in my eyes, sharp and immediate, but it didn't hurt the way I expected. Because his restraint felt like respect, not rejection.

"I know," I whispered. "I'm not mad. I can't be. You told me what it was, so to let it go this far was on me."

His thumb brushed my cheek and trailed down to my lips. "This celibacy thing used to be easy for me until I met you," he said. "I promised God I wouldn't touch the right woman at the wrong time."

"I understand, Reid. Trust me, I do," I said softly.

His eyes searched mine. "This is harder for me than you think. But I can't break promises I made to God. He's been too good to me."

Something inside me fell off the shelf. "I think," I said, my voice barely steady, "I hope you don't look at me like a bad person. I know that you were close with Jahi, and you're probably thinking that I'm moving on extremely fast, considering it was just a short time ago that my husband expired. But the truth is, he forced me out of love a long time ago."

He didn't say anything. He sat there, listening, hanging on every word.

I continued, "Yes, I loved him, but I hadn't been in love with him in forever. I know that if I were to start dating now, people would think I moved on quickly, but the truth is, I moved on a long time ago. Just not on paper. I wanted to leave him, but because of who he was, and who he represented, I didn't want to bring a scandal to our family. People in our family don't get divorced. They just sit in it until one of them dies. I never wished death on my husband, but I can't say that I am as broken as some people probably think I am. I said all of that to say this, I think...I think I like you more than I should." The words scared me the moment they left my mouth.

He didn't pull away the way I thought he would. Instead, he kissed my forehead slowly.

"Then we slow this down," he said. "And we protect it."

We separated after that, not because the want disappeared, but because it mattered too much to let it run wild. He walked me to my bedroom door like it was sacred ground, stopped, and looked at me once more like he was committing me to memory.

"Goodnight, Nuri."

"Goodnight, Reid."

When the door closed behind me, I leaned against it,

heart racing, body still buzzing, and the feel of his lips still lingered across my skin.

Outside my room, danger still waited. Mercury still watched, and truth still lurked in the shadows. But inside me, something had taken root. Something fragile and powerful.

And I knew...without a doubt...falling for Reid might be the most dangerous thing I'd done yet.

Chapter Seventeen

The call came at 6:17 a.m., and that's how I knew things weren't ok. Nobody calls with good news at that hour. Especially not in Atlanta. Not in my life. I rolled over to my phone lighting up on the nightstand. Paige's name was flashing like she was screaming at me. I answered before the second ring. Somehow, I already knew this had something to do with Mercury...because everything did now.

"Nuri," she said, breathless. She wasn't loud, and she wasn't playing like she always does. That shit scared me more than if she'd been yelling.

"What's up? What's going on?"

"What's going on is I'm at Grady. Somebody attacked Maya," she cried.

The word attacked didn't register at first. It hovered a minute before it landed.

"What do you mean she's been attacked?" I asked, my voice suddenly shaky.

"They jumped her outside her building. She was leaving her house for work. She's conscious but bruised badly. They left her with a stab wound to the shoulder."

My stomach churned so hard I thought I might be sick.

"A stab wound?!?!" I screamed. "I'm on my way," I said, already moving.

I ran into the guest room where Reid was asleep. His eyes popped open before I even touched him. I didn't have to explain. He saw the look on my face, and that was enough. Within minutes, we were in the car, Atlanta sliding past us so quickly it looked like streaks. I wanted to say something, but I couldn't. I didn't know what to say. I glanced over at Reid. He was grinding his teeth with his hands steady on the wheel, his eyes scanning every intersection before making a turn. I watched his body language and realized he was just as angry as I was.

At the hospital, Maya looked so fragile. The fact that my friend...soft spoken, church going, never wronged anybody...was lying in a bed with bruises blossoming across her skin almost sent me into a panic attack. She was wrapped in a thin blanket. Her eyes were swollen shut with bandages on her shoulder and arm, IV taped to her hand. She tried to smile when she saw me, and I tried to do the same.

"I'm okay," she whispered.

I nodded, even though nothing was okay. I kissed her forehead, swallowed the rage climbing my throat, and stroked her hair. Charity stood near the wall with her arms folded tight. Her jaw was clenched so hard I thought it might crack. Paige was pacing with furious tears sliding down her face.

"Maya, did you see who did this to you?" I asked.

Charity shook her head. "No, she didn't. They had on a hoodie, gloves, and a mask. That shit sounded real intentional to me."

Reid's posture shifted beside me. "This wasn't random," he said quietly.

"No shit," Paige snapped. "All I need to know is who's responsible for this shit. Do you two know? Is there something you need to tell us, Nuri?"

"I guess it is. Look, I've been having some really strange things happening around my house. Things left on my car, strange ass voicemails, and indirect threats. They've been fucking with me for a minute now, but I never imagined it would come to this."

Rolling her eyes, Paige muttered, "Don't you think

that was something you should have told us? Maybe warned us a little. I mean damn, Nuri."

"I'm sorry. I honestly didn't think I needed to mention it. It had nothing to do with you all. It's me he wants. Not you," I said.

"Obviously you were wrong. You have some damn lunatic after you, and you didn't even warn us. You're no better than Jahi," Paige spat.

"Now hold the fuck on, Paige. I just told you—"

"Wait, everyone. Stop yelling," Reid barked. "This is not the time or place. I understand emotions are high because of what happened with Maya, but this isn't anyone's fault but the person responsible. Nuri didn't ask for any of this just like Maya didn't. So can you all please calm down?"

Paige sucked in a deep breath. "You're right. I'm sorry, Nuri. I shouldn't have said that shit. I'm heated as fuck, and I want to rock somebody's shit for what happened to Maya. She didn't deserve this. She doesn't bother anybody. Now, tell me...who do you think did this?"

My chest felt hollow as the name crawled up my throat.

Mercury.

I didn't need to explain. Everyone in that room already knew his name.

"I know you aren't talking about that pretty ass boy

that's always at the local charities with his fake philanthropic bullshit. The one that's always talking about what he's doing for the community, but everybody knows that he's been scamming and slanging dope for years."

"Yes, that's him," I quipped.

"What does he have to do with any of this?" Charity asked. "Was Jahi entangled with him in some kind of way?"

Before I could answer, Maya began to stir. Her voice barely a whisper. "They said...tell Nuri...to stop."

That was it. That was the message. After that statement, we didn't stay long. The doctors needed space, Maya needed her rest, and I needed air before I shattered. I gave her a kiss, apologized once again, and said my goodbyes before leaving.

The drive back felt longer than the drive to the hospital. The closer we got, the heavier my chest felt, like the air itself was warning me.

Reid pulled into the driveway and stopped short. The front door was closed but disturbed. Not forced open, not broken, just disturbed.

My heart started pounding. "Reid."

"I see it," he said.

He went in first with his weapon drawn, body shifting around walls. He was all business. I waited outside on the porch until he gave me the ok to enter. My mouth hung open as I stepped across the threshold. Standing in the foyer, I almost couldn't recognize my own home. The house looked like it had been rummaged through by someone impatient. Shit was everywhere. Drawers pulled out but not emptied. Files scattered but not taken. Couch cushions slashed open like someone had lost patience halfway through searching them. The office looked like a paper storm had hit it...documents everywhere, desk overturned, safe wide open and insultingly untouched.

They hadn't wanted money. They wanted knowledge.

"They were looking for something specific," Reid said, still moving through the rooms, checking corners, windows, shadows. "And they didn't find it."

A cold chill crept up my spine. "How did they get past the cameras and the security system? I didn't get any kind of alert on my phone. Did you?"

"No, I didn't either. They must've cut the main frame. Whoever's responsible knows what they're doing."

"That was a message," I said.

"Yes," he agreed. "And I'm about sick and tired of these fucking messages. It's time for me to turn the voicemail off," he whispered with a cold look in his eyes.

My phone buzzed. It was an unknown number. I answered because I knew it had to be the piece of shit responsible for this. No one else had such perfect timing.

"Your friend has a beautiful relationship with the man

above. She prayed to him and begged for her life so beautifully," a voice muttered. Smooth and calm.

"Fuck you, Mercury!! Whoever you send to attack my friend is a fucking coward. Just like you. She had nothing to do with anything. None of them do. You want me, so why are you fucking with them?" I yelled into the phone.

"If I were you, I'd show a little gratitude. She's alive," he continued. "That's your mercy. Don't mistake it for weakness."

"What do you want?" I demanded, voice shaking.

A pause. Then—

"Your father had a small...incident late last night. I'm surprised your mother didn't call and tell you, or maybe she did and you ignored her."

The world tilted as the words poured from his lips.

"What incident?"

"He collapsed during an impromptu meeting," Mercury said lightly. "Stress does terrible things to the body. He's alive. For now."

Reid's hand closed around mine.

"This shit needs to end now," I said, my voice breaking. "I don't know who in the fuck you think you are, but you should really stick to scamming, you worthless piece of shit. You don't get to keep touching my life like this and get away with it."

He let out a soft chuckle. "You misunderstand, Mrs.

Laurent," Mercury replied. "I already own pieces of it. I just wanted to make sure you understood how many."

The line went dead.

I stood there in the wreckage of my home, my best friend in a hospital bed, my father suddenly vulnerable, and understood the truth with brutal clarity: Mercury wanted to dismantle my world, one person at a time, and he needed to be stopped before he got that satisfaction.

I shook off my anger and quickly placed a call to my mother. She answered on the first ring.

"So, you finally decide to reach out to me. I've been calling you for weeks, and all you've done is send me to voicemail. Just who in the hell do you think you are?"

I took a deep breath to center myself before speaking. "I'm sorry, Mother. I'm still processing. I've been in a mood, and instead of projecting my feelings onto others, I've been avoiding the phone. I called you because I got word that Daddy had some kind of incident. Is he ok?"

"Looks like someone was able to reach you because I sure as hell couldn't. How did you find out about your father?"

"None of that matters. What matters is that Dad is ok. Is he ok? May I speak with him?"

"He's been better, and he's resting. I'll have him call you when he awakes."

She hung up.

Chapter Eighteen

"You funky bitch," I whispered as the line went dead, and my blood pressure rose. I wish I could say I couldn't believe she hung up in my face, but her disrespecting me was a common occurrence. She never gave a damn about me or my feelings. Instead of waiting to receive a call from my father, I grabbed my keys off the hook and headed towards the garage. Reid was on my heels.

"I'm not going to ask you where you're going because I know," he quipped, his hands on his hips. "But you know I can't allow you to go alone. Let me make sure no one is in this home and lock up, and we can leave. How does that sound?"

"That's fine, but can you make it quick? Please hurry up, Reid," I shouted as I raised the garage door. I sat in the driver's side waiting on him to return. Looking in my vanity mirror at myself, I almost felt sick to my stomach. Not because of the woman that stared back at me, but because of what my life had become...chaos. I never liked chaos. Peace was more my speed, but it felt like peace was becoming a distant memory.

"Reid, what is taking you so long? I'm leaving you here if you don't hurry up," I screamed from the driver's side of my Benz. Coming out the door with his forehead wrinkled, he opened the car door and plopped down.

"Nuri, in all the time that you've known me...have you known me to rush, get in a hurry, or jump when someone says jump? I'll answer that for you. No. I understand you are upset and anxious about all the shit going on around you, but you've got to keep a calm head. Especially with me. I don't do too well with being yelled at. Now, please exit the vehicle and come around to the passenger side. I'm driving, and I'm not taking no for an answer," he mumbled as he opened the passenger door and walked to the driver's side. "There is no way you're about to chauffeur me anywhere with that attitude."

I shrugged my shoulders, and I did what I was told.

"Are you happy now?" I scowled.

"No, but I'm better now that you're over there and I'm over here. Please put the address in the GPS so we can be on our way."

"If you had let me stay where I was, there would be no need for any of this." I smacked my lips as I typed my mother's address into the navigation system.

"Nuri, you can talk until you're blue in the face, and it won't change anything. I will get you where you need to go, safe and sound, and make sure you return home the same way. Then you can go your way, and I will go mine. Still in the same house, of course. I can tell you're having a hard time dealing with all this, but I'm not about to let you turn me into a punching bag. I'll just stay out of your way until you're feeling better."

He cranked the car and pulled out of the driveway. He was eerily silent for most of the ride. I glanced over at him; his jaw was tight, and he was deep in thought. The silence was gnawing at me as each mile passed. I knew I was wrong to take out my frustrations on the one person that had been down with me from the very beginning. I'd never been too good to admit when I'm wrong.

Turning to him to apologize, I cleared my throat and grabbed his hand. "Reid, I'm sorry. I shouldn't have yelled at you like that back at the house. I've got so much on my mind, and if I'm being honest with you, I'm overwhelmed, and apparently, I'm not handling it very well."

"I know, Nuri. Which is the very reason I haven't snatched your little ass up. Don't get me wrong...I would never hit or hurt you in any way, but I sure as hell will pin your little ass down until you surrender and stop your foolishness." He removed my hand from his and placed it back on the wheel.

True, I was worried about my father, but his statement completely derailed my thought process. The combination of the look on his face, the fire in his eyes, and the tone in his voice sent a wave straight to my yoni. His words were firm, and I knew he was serious. Yet all I could think of was his tongue lapping at my clit. Those big firm hands wrapped around my throat and me surrendering to his every whim.

I crossed my legs. He noticed, and I attempted to change the subject.

"Reid, the house is a mess. Do you think I should hire someone to come clean and reorganize? I can do it myself, but it would take ages. All those drawers and file cabinets have to be rearranged. Oh, and we're going to have to hit up a furniture store for new furniture. They ruined the sofas."

"We...so you're speaking French now? Nuri, that is your house. You can decorate it any way you like."

He was right, but somehow his statement hurt my feelings. Not wanting to let it show...I continued. "You're right. It is my house. I can do what I want with it. Everything in that house was picked out by Jahi. None of it is my style at all. If I'm going to remain there, and that's a big if..., I have to make it more me, less him."

Reid looked at me and inhaled deeply before setting his eyes back on the road. "Like I said, Nuri, do what you want. It's none of my business."

"I said I was sorry, Reid. Why do you still have an attitude with me? I know I was wrong and admitted it. What more do you want?"

"I want to get you to your father and return back to your house. It's not you, and I'm not angry. I don't get angry. I'm just tired of this shit already. This man has been running us ragged with his bullshit, and it doesn't seem to be slowing down. Looks like I'm going to have to slow it down myself. The way I know how. This muthafucka has had someone come to your house and try to intimidate you. He had someone hurt one of your dearest friends, and now he's come to the house where I currently lay my head and ransacked it. This shit can't slide any longer. I'm going to put an end to this shit, and I mean quickly." His hands tightened around the wheel.

Just as I was about to speak up, the navigation system began to announce, "You've arrived at your destination."

Our eyes met as he exited the car before coming around and opening my door. I hopped out and pulled him close to me. "Reid, you are about to meet the horrid individual I call my mother in person. I need to take the opportunity and warn you; she's a handful and a certified man eater. She will ask inappropriate questions, she will make assumptions, and it's a high probability you may leave here pissed. Please know, none of that is a reflection of me. I'm nothing like her."

"I know, Nuri. You don't need to give me a disclaimer. I heard her on the phone, and I saw her in action at the party. You have to remember; I was in the Marine Corps for many years. I'm used to dealing with people like her, and what she does won't phase me one way or the other," he said confidently.

He flashed a slight smile my way and escorted me to the door.

"Here goes nothing," I said as I rang the doorbell. Within seconds, the door flew open, and my mother appeared with an annoyed look on her face.

"What are you doing here?" she scowled.

"Hello to you too, Mother. I came to check on Daddy. I wanted to make sure he's good and see if there is anything I can do for him."

Smacking her lips, she spat, "You can't do anything more than I can do. It's not like you have any professional medical training so I don't need your help. I told you he was resting, and I would call when he woke up. I don't appreciate you coming by without calling. I don't care if he is your father. I taught you better than to show up unannounced at people's houses," she said as she stepped outside the door. "And who is this tall drink of water?" she asked as she cut her eyes at Reid. "He's fine, but Nuri, don't you think it's still a bit early for you to start dating? Jahi's damn head isn't cold yet, and you are already on the damn prowl." She chuckled proudly and continued, "All that other shit you do is annoying, but this...you got from me, 'cause baby, I loves me a tall, chocolate sexy ass man." Reid turned away as she looked him up and down.

"It's not what you think. Mom, this is Reid. He's my security."

"Sure he is. He can secure me anytime," she whispered in a low, sexy voice.

"Mama, that is not appropriate. You are a married woman, and not just a married woman, but a woman married to my father. Stop acting like some bitch in heat," I spat.

Her eyes darkened. Before I could apologize, she raised her hand and slapped my face so hard...I thought she'd knocked out a tooth.

Gritting her teeth, she said, "As long as you are on this earth, you will never speak to me that way again. And if you do, I will put you next to your husband. Do you understand me?"

I didn't say a word. I wanted to rock her shit, but I let

her have it. I ate the punch, my feelings, and my words in hopes she would let me in.

"I'm sorry, Mother. I shouldn't have said that, and I apologize. I also apologize for popping up, but I didn't think I needed an invitation to visit my father. I've never needed one before." I bucked my eyes at her, but she didn't budge. "Are you going to let me in or no? Even if I don't talk to him, I would like to lay eyes on him."

"That's not happening. Now, you and Mr. Reid can get off my doorstep and trot back across town to the mansion that has your name on it. This one does not. I'm not letting you in, and that's final," she said as she took a step back inside and slammed the door.

Livid and completely helpless, I stood there for a minute before I turned and faced Reid.

"Please get me the fuck out of here before I burst every window in this tacky ass house. Why does she hate me so much? I don't deserve to be treated like this. No one does. Here I am, trying to be a good daughter and see if she needs any help caring for my father, and the bitch won't even let me see him."

A single tear fell from my eye as Reid gently grabbed my wrist before sweeping my hair behind my ear.

"I think this is deeper than your mother not liking or caring for you. It's more than that. Has to be, but we can discuss that later. Let's get you out of here. You are too much of a lady to stay somewhere you're not wanted."

Placing his hand at the small of my back, he gently nudged me forward. Reluctantly, I began to move. I wanted to shake him and run back towards the door, but I knew deep down inside, it wouldn't have done any good. My mother had been known to die on many hills.

The tears kept rolling once we were back in the car. I fought them tooth and nail, but they were relentless. I lost. I was drowning in worry and fear, and I didn't anticipate it ending anytime soon.

Pulling me from my thoughts, Reid placed his hand on my thigh. The way your man does when he wants to reassure you everything's going to be ok. It didn't work, but his touch felt phenomenal.

"It's early. Neither one of us has eaten, and we have a lot to handle once we return back to the house. Would you like to grab a bite to eat before we head back?" Reid asked while pulling into Denny's.

"Why ask me if you were going to make the decision for me?" I queried.

"Because I have manners, and it was the proper thing to do, but I knew you would say yes. Your ass is not about to turn down good food," he chuckled.

He was right. I was just glad he chose somewhere low key and not fancy. I was sick and tired of those hoity-toity restaurants Jahi loved to frequent. No flavor, no vibe, no soul. Tasteless dishes with superb service. I'd settle for shitty service if the food is banging, and the Grand Slam never failed me.

Sauntering into the restaurant made me think of the golden days. The days when I'd just moved out of my mother's house and was being a big girl all on my own. When I barely had two nickels to rub together because I refused to ask my parents for anything. Days when I would work the morning shift at the YMCA and turn around and work the night shift at the hotel doing night audits.

As we walked further inside, the delicious smell of pancakes and bacon filled the air, and my stomach growled with excitement.

"Damn girl, you really are hungry. I heard that," Reid said before walking in front of me and addressing the hostess. "Ma'am, would you happen to have any seats in the back away from the windows?"

She nodded yes as she grabbed two menus and ushered us to the back of the restaurant. We were promptly seated as Reid took the seat facing the entrance and gestured me to the other side. Placing our orders, we sat quietly until the waitress returned with our food.

"What are you thinking about, Nuri?"

"My father," I answered. "I wonder how he's feeling. If he knows who's responsible for his incident? Hell, I still don't know what the incident is. I'm just as lost as they come."

"I know all this is hard, but I promise you, everything is going to be ok. Even your father. I'll make sure of it. If you'd like, I can put someone on him to make sure no one can harm him. Help is only a phone call away. I've got a team of guys just as good as me, and they will watch him from a distance. You know...like I did with you."

"You would do that for me?"

"Of course I would. Once we get back to the house, I'll set it up for you and get the ball rolling. You said money wasn't a problem, and I hope you were serious because around-the-clock surveillance isn't cheap."

"If it will keep my parents safe, then I don't care what the cost is. I'll cover it." I inhaled deeply, then took a bite of my eggs and continued. "Everything around me is coming apart at the seams. I can't help but take some kind of blame even though I've done nothing."

Reid looked up and shook his head no at me. "Exactly...you've done nothing, so why are you taking responsibility for something you had no part in?" Reid offered. "It's not your fault that these men have no integrity or moral compass. They don't care who they hurt as long as they come out on top. That's on them. That has nothing to do with Nuri. Remember that."

"I'm trying, Reid, but let me tell you what's troubling

me the most. These people want something from me, but they won't come out and say exactly what it is. Instead, they are running around here making all this noise. Wrecking shit, threatening and attacking people, and for what? They don't even know themselves. All they know is they want my mouth shut, but they have no proof that I know anything. Just a bunch of people on a power trip, scared their secrets might come out."

"If you think about it, it makes no sense. Yes, Jahi discovered secrets, but he hadn't told anyone what he'd discovered or if he discovered anything. According to him, I'm the only one who knows. They are literally harassing me over what-ifs, and in my opinion, that's stupid as hell. I mean, if I were them, I'd leave me the fuck alone because if you keep fucking with the bull, you eventually get the horns. I don't bother anybody, and I never have, but they are going to make me go off my medicine, and then I'd really give them something to worry about."

Reid chuckled as he took the last bite of that tough ass steak he was eating.

"Nuri, what do you mean go off your medicine?"

"Exactly what I said. I take a large dose of happy pills every morning. I have since I was fourteen years old. I was diagnosed with depression as a teen, and without my medicine, I'm as angry as a wet hen. If you want to know why... just think about my interaction with my mother back at her house. Imagine dealing with that every day of your life. You'd be on medicine too."

"Oh, I'm not judging," Reid uttered. "They tried to put me on medicine once I left the military, but I prefer to deal with my stress in other ways."

"Yeah, me too. My main go-to was masturbation, but if I kept that up, I was for sure going to go blind. I mean, I was flicking my bean so much that one time I thought I broke it."

Reid cracked up laughing while signaling the waitress for the check.

"Come on, girl. Let me get your crazy ass back home so we can get this house together."

Chapter Nineteen

Once we arrived back in the driveway, Reid performed a sweep of the grounds before entering the house. He told me to stay in the car until he came back to get me. A feeling of dread started to wash over me as I waited for him to return. I sat and contemplated whether it was a good idea for me to enter into my own home. My mind was telling me no, and to get away. When he returned to the car, I refused to get out.

"Nuri, I checked every square inch of the inside as well as the outside. We're all good. You can come on in," he said as he opened the car door.

Grabbing the door handle, I closed it back.

"I don't want to go in there. I want to leave. I don't care where we go. I just don't wanna be here."

"Are you serious right now? Correct me if I'm wrong,

but aren't you the one that said you weren't going to run? That you were going to stand tall?"

"Reid, I know what I said, but that was before one of my best friends was stabbed and my father attacked. I don't think it's safe for you or me to return until we can get this situation under control. And I'm not running. I just need to get away for a few and think."

"Nuri, sweetheart, I understand that you're scared, but is it really worth you leaving your own home?" He shifted his stance toward the house while waiting on an answer.

"Reid," I snapped. "I said I don't feel safe, so I want to leave. Please don't take this the wrong way, but I'm not so certain anymore that you can protect me. They were able to gain access to my home and rummage through my belongings. I feel violated, and I want to get the fuck out of here. I don't give a shit about this house or the shit in it. Now let's go, please."

"Hey, you're the boss, and if you want to leave, we will leave. Do you have somewhere in particular in mind?" Reid asked. I could tell he was frustrated by my rash decision-making, but I paid him to do. Not think.

"I do. I own a property in Barbados. Jahi and I vacationed there once, and I loved it so much that we decided to purchase a residence. We can go there. I just need a little time to handle the logistics, and we should be able to leave within a few hours."

"I'm down with that. Before we leave, I need to stop by my place to sew up a little business and get some things in order. Not to mention, set up your father's security detail. You can come with me if you want, or I can drop you off at one of your girls' houses until I return."

"I'll come with you. I don't think I'm their favorite person right now. Especially not after what was done to Maya. I could tell they blamed me for what happened to her, and if I'm being honest with myself... I blame me too. Anyway, lock up the house, turn the security system back on, and we can leave now."

"Damn. You're really serious about getting out of here. Are you not going to pack anything? I've never known a woman to travel without at least three suitcases."

"No, as I said, I don't want to go back into the house right now. The house in Barbados has everything I need, and what it doesn't have, I will buy when we get there. You can go in there if you want and get your things, but I'm good."

He stood there for a moment, blankly looking into the sky, like he was trying to decide. I didn't want him to think too hard on it, so I decided for him.

"Do you have your gun on you?" I asked.

"Of course I do. You know I don't move without it."

"Do you also have extra magazines?"

"I do," he retorted.

"Good. That's all you need. Get in the car. Let's go."

He ran back to the house, locked up, and trekked back to the car. We drove through Atlanta, traffic moving in every direction at once. Being in the city felt too loud now. Engines roared, sirens blared, and the sound of people weaving in and out of traffic had my anxiety on high. Red lights came too quickly. Billboards, storefronts, crowded overpasses, and the skyline never forgot to let me know where I was.

Then the roads narrowed into two-lane roads edged with trees. The traffic dropped almost suddenly. Gas stations and flea markets disappeared and were replaced by stretches of forest and open sky. The air felt different. It was calmer. It was still. Miles passed without seeing another car, and the pavement winded through farmland and low hills. Eventually, even the houses fell away. Finally, Reid turned onto a private road, barely marked. Gravel crunched beneath the tires. Acres of land opened up on both sides. A fishing pond sat out to the left. The land felt uninterrupted and still, like a small oasis of peace. There were no neighboring rooftops or streetlights. Just trees, grass, and the beautiful view of nature.

The house revealed itself gradually. It was set back and unassuming at first glance. A modest mansion of pale stone and soft lines. The grounds were beautifully kept. Broad lawns, mature trees, with carefully placed shrubs and hedges. We arrived without fanfare, but I knew immediately he'd taken me somewhere special.

As the car slowly rolled to a stop in front of the mansion, Reid turned to me. "I've never discussed this part of my life with you, and normally I wouldn't, but considering the circumstances, I need to. This is my home that I share with my mother. She has ALS. I moved her here with me right after she was diagnosed. I am her primary caretaker... well, me along with the nurses that see about her when I'm not available because of work. My mom has around-the-clock care.

"Whenever you see me duck off and make a phone call, that's usually me calling to check on her. Her disease has progressed, so she can no longer speak, but I know she's still in there. So you see, I have responsibilities and a business to run too. However, I promised to be there for you. I won't desert you because you need me, but she does too. I said that to say this... yes, I agreed to protect you and accompany you on your getaway, as I know you need to get yourself together, but if someone calls and tells me I'm needed back home, I'm on the first thing smoking. No questions asked. I will arrange a replacement for me if need be. That's if you're not ready to return to the states just yet. My mother is my everything, and I love her beyond measure. She is one of the most important people in my life, so please be sure this is what you want before those wheels go up."

"Yes, I understand, and I don't blame you. I would do the same. I finally get to meet the woman that birthed the rigid-ass man I stare at today?"

"I resent that. I'm not rigid, and yes, you get to meet my beautiful mother," he smirked.

As soon as we walked to the door, the house came alive. The groundskeeper stepped forward first, hat in hand. "Mr. Mercer."

Behind him, the house manager appeared, tablet tucked against her chest, expression calm but alert. And then the nurses—two of them—moved quickly toward the front steps, their presence quiet but urgent.

I watched him shift. The man who had stood beside me in hospitals and chaos, who carried danger in his silence, softened in a way I had never seen.

"Morning update?" he asked one of the nurses.

"She slept through the night," the nurse said gently. "No respiratory distress. Appetite was minimal, but she responded well to therapy this morning. Her mood has been... brighter."

Reid nodded once, absorbing every word like it mattered more than anything else in the world.

"Thank you."

He turned to me. "Come."

Not an order. An invitation.

We moved through the house together. Our footsteps clicked against marble floors and quiet hallways. The estate was beautiful, but it didn't feel like a home. It felt like a sanctuary built around something special.

Reid stopped outside a bedroom door. For a second, he didn't open it. I realized then that this wasn't fear. It was reverence.

Inside, the room was filled with soft light and the faint hum of medical equipment. His mother sat propped up in bed, her body was thinner than I imagined, her hands resting lightly beautiful crochet blanket. When she saw him, her face changed and her eyes lit up. Reid crossed the room in three strides and took her hand carefully, as if she were made of glass.

"Hey, Mom," he said quietly.

She couldn't speak. The disease had stolen her voice, her strength, her independence. But it hadn't stolen her love. Her fingers tightened around his as tears filled her eyes. She smiled. Reid bent down and pressed a kiss to her forehead, then another to her temple. His hand never left hers.

"I know," he murmured. "I missed you too."

Something inside my chest cracked.

He pulled a chair closer and sat beside her, their hands still joined. For a moment, the world outside that room didn't exist. No Mercury. No danger or secrets. Hell, I was in the room, and I didn't matter. It was just a son and his mother.

Then he turned slightly, glancing at me.

"Mom," he said softly, "this is Nuri."

His mother's gaze shifted to me. Reid squeezed her hand gently.

"She's important to me."

Her eyes studied me, not with suspicion, but with warmth. Slowly, with effort, she lifted her free hand and reached toward me. I stepped forward without thinking. Her fingers brushed mine. The touch was light, trembling, but so very sweet.

Reid smiled.

"She's going to be around for a while," he said.

His mother's eyes shimmered. And suddenly I couldn't breathe. Because she was showing him love without words, without conditions, without hesitation. And my own mother had never once looked at me like that.

Reid leaned closer to his mother again. "I'm going out of town for a little while," he told her gently. "Business."

Her fingers tightened again, just slightly.

"But you're in the best hands," he continued. "The nurses. The staff. Everything is covered as always, and as you know, I'm only a phone call away."

He brushed his thumb over her knuckles.

"And if you need me," he said, voice low but certain, "I'll be there. Always."

She stared at him with a smile spread across her face. They sat like that for a long moment. Hand in hand. Heart to heart. Love so visible it almost hurt to witness.

I felt tears on my own face before I realized I was crying. Quietly, I stepped back. They didn't notice when I left. I found my way to the courtyard. Outside, the air felt different. The grounds stretched wide and far. It was immaculate.

I walked slowly, letting the silence wrap around me. My chest ached. Not with jealousy, but with grief. Because somewhere deep inside, I understood something I had never allowed myself to name:

Reid had been loved. Adored. And I had grown up in a house where love felt like punishment.

I stopped near a fountain, staring at the water, and wondered what it would feel like to be loved the way he was.

Chapter Twenty

I made my way back inside, where I found Reid still cuddled comfortably next to his mother. Not wanting to interrupt their time together, I trekked back to the car to wait while he finished things up. The second my ass sat firmly onto the seat, my notifications went off. There was no frantic buzzing or messages at rapid successions. Just a single ding from an unknown number. Here we go again, I whispered to myself.

I opened it to find a photo. For a moment, my brain refused to comprehend what my eyes were clearly seeing. The lighting was soft and intimate, and there was a woman stretched across crisp white sheets. Her body turned just enough that there was no mistaking her vulnerability, her comfort, and her lack of shame.

My Mother

Her features were unmistakable even when her face was partially covered. She was relaxed in a way I'd never seen before. This wasn't a stolen or accidental moment. This was a moment she fully participated in. She allowed it to exist. My stomach dropped as another message followed immediately.

> Unknown number: We all have leverage, Nuri. Yours just happens to be... sentimental.

My hands started shaking as I scrolled. There were more images. At first, nothing too explicit, although seeing my mother in this light was still too raunchy for my eyes. While they weren't explicit, they were indeed intimate. Her jewelry was laid out on a nightstand that I didn't recognize. There sat a familiar bracelet. One that always adorned her wrist, along with a white gold and diamond cross my father gifted years back. Then, a video was delivered along with a message.

> Unknown number: I hope you're sitting down. This is just the tip of the iceberg. This is the kind of blood you have running through your veins.

This is when my pulse really kicked up. With my eyes slightly cracked, I pressed play only to find my mother taking backshots while giving someone head. I almost fainted in the car. The air was too thin. I hopped out and walked around to sit on the hood. In that moment, I wished I could be surprised, but I wasn't. Disgusted, yes. Surprised, no. My mother had been known to sleep around. Everyone at the company and on the social scene seemed to be aware. Everyone but my father.

Then the last message came through, and it knocked me out my heels.

> Unknown number: Aht, aht, don't close it back. Trust me, you want to see it to the end.

Opening my phone back up, I fast-forwarded until the fucking of my mother's parts ceased and the camera panned to the man that was receiving head. There, in all his glory and splendor, stood my husband. My husband and Mercury both were fucking my mother.

My heart felt as if it was melting inside my body. No matter how deep the breaths I took, I wasn't getting enough air. I doubled over in front of the car, and just as I was about to fall, I felt Reid's hand reach for mine and try to pull me up. When he couldn't, he picked me up like I weighed as much as a feather and brought me back into the house.

Sitting me on the couch, he muttered, "Nuri, talk to me, please. Tell me what's going on."

There wasn't enough air in my lungs to answer, so I handed him my phone. I watched his expression change as he took in the images. It wasn't shock displayed across his face...Reid didn't do shock, but something else. Confusion.

"Ummm, am I tripping, or is this your mother and your dead husband in this video?" he questioned.

I mustered up enough energy and air to respond. "Yes, along with Mercury giving my mother backshots."

"And he sent this to you?"

"Yes."

Reid exhaled slowly. "You do realize he's escalating."

My laugh came out thin and disbelieving. "This is humiliating."

The phone rang while still in Reid's hands. He was about to answer, but I pleaded with him to let me instead. He handed over the phone without protest.

I couldn't let him know I was shaken. I steadied my voice and answered as calmly as I could. "Just what in the fuck are you trying to prove? What is it that you want? Tell me and stop playing these games because I don't have time for them. You're doing all this shit for what, Mercury?"

His voice came through, even and chilling. "I thought you'd appreciate knowing what your body will look like in about thirty years. Not bad, if I do say so myself. I'm sure if Jahi was alive, he'd agree. Since he isn't, I'll do him a solid and answer for him. She still has lots of fire left and sucks a mean dick, as you can see. She takes as good as she gives," he chuckled.

My chest burned.

"Your mother has always been concerned about appearances. Back down before Atlanta gets an education about her history of being a pass-around slut."

Sucking my teeth, I shot back, "Back down from what, Mercury? I haven't done shit but live and mind my business. You are the one fucking with me and mine, and you're telling me to back down. What is it you think I know? Because I can assure you, I don't know shit."

"I'm not stupid, Nuri. Jahi found out about the Greystone Project and was about to spill the beans. I have a lot of money tied up in that project, and I'm not about to let you or anyone else fuck that up. And I don't believe you didn't know. As close as you and him were, there's no way he didn't tell you."

"So he had you fooled too, huh?" I chuckled. "For your information, Jahi never shared his business endeavors with me. Never. I don't even know what the Greystone Project is. Should I know?"

"Are you telling me this man laid next to your fine ass

every night and never told you about the shit he was into?" Mercury asked.

"That's exactly what I'm telling you. For the past two years, Jahi and I slept in separate bedrooms. When he was home, we barely spoke to one another. Our relationship was far from perfect, but that was what he wanted everyone to believe. We weren't perfect at all. Truthfully, I wanted to divorce him, and he wanted me to disappear, so the last thing we were doing was pillow talking. I'm telling you now, you can stop this bullshit because I have no idea what he was into, and I certainly don't know what you were into either."

The phone went silent for a moment.

"If you are lying to me and if my name is brought up in anything... you will see me again, and this time you will feel me. Do you understand?"

"I understand you are like most men. Instead of simply talking to me, you took the bitch way out and tried to dismantle my life. Now you see it was for nothing, and I bet you feel stupid as fuck—and if not, you should."

"No," he snapped. "I bet *you* feel stupid as fuck to see your husband's dick in your mother's mouth. Like I said, if my name or any of my companies are mentioned in any scandal, I will air your mother's whore ass out. The church, the board members, and that feeble-ass husband will be done with her. Her name won't mean shit in these Atlanta streets."

"Whatever, Mercury. Are we done? Like really done? Is the retrograde over? Because I can't take any more of this bullshit. I'm tired, and I want to heal and move on with my life. Whatever shit you have going on has nothing to do with me."

The line went dead.

Reid turned to me. "I heard everything. You handled that very well. I'm impressed."

"Thank you. It did sound like he fell for it, didn't he? I hope he did. Maybe now I can breathe a little easier."

"Nope... don't count him out yet. I'm willing to bet good money he will still have someone watching you. It's too soon to know, but men like that are always suspicious of everyone. As for those pictures and videos... that had to be hard to see. Are you okay?"

"No, I'm not. I'm sick to my stomach. My mother was fucking my husband. I knew she hated me, but damn. This is diabolical."

"I agree, Nuri. It is. If I had children, I could never imagine doing something like that to them. It takes a real piece of shit to go after your child's husband. Anyhow, since you and Mercury are supposedly squared away, do you still want to go to Barbados?"

"Hell yes, I do. Him agreeing to leave me alone doesn't change the fact that I want to get the fuck away from Atlanta. Especially now. That's the only thing that will stop me from heading back across town and breaking my foot off in my mother's ass," I spat.

"The funny thing is, he sent you a video of your mother betraying you in one of the worst ways possible, then expected you to protect her. That in itself is bananas. This is the type of shit you can't make up," he chuckled. "Some men really are dumb as hell."

"Yes, some women too. The crazy thing is, my mother has spent her life controlling narratives, curating power, selling respectability like a drug. And he was holding her secrets like weapons. He thought he would use her body, her reputation, her fear as leverage against me." I straightened. "He doesn't know her the way I do."

Reid's eyes sharpened. "Meaning."

"Meaning... she will burn everything down to protect her own image. Including him. He thought he was finding my weak spot, but I found his, along with the truth. He did indeed have his hand in the cookie jar, but it wasn't in there alone. He doesn't work for the company, so he had to gain his knowledge through someone else. Someone internally had to put him on. Who that other person was, I don't know, but I will find out one way or another. Shit, my husband and I were not on the best terms, but he was still my husband. He died for this shit. Money and info. It's so fucked up."

Reid shifted his stance as he took a seat next to me. Sick of talking about Mercury and my mother, I changed the subject.

"Anyhow, is your mother good?"

"Yes, Mom is fine. Better than fine, actually. She knows I'm still at her beck and call, but it will take a little while to get to her if need be. Hopefully, nothing happens while I'm away. She's been doing well these last few months. This is the only reason I'm comfortable with leaving her a little while. Otherwise, I'd have to tell that beautiful caramel colored face of yours no." He looked deep into my eyes as he cupped my face. "And Lord knows I hate to tell you no."

"In that case, are you ready to roll, Mr. Mercer?"

"I am. I've already left the staff with your information and mine. I've given Mother all the kisses she could handle, and your parent's detail is ready to go—or would you like me to call them off?" He stared at me as he tried to hold back his laugh.

"No," I smiled. "My father still deserves protection. Just like Mercury still may not trust me, I sure as hell don't trust him. Just have them know they don't have to guard my mother so closely. A few buckshots in her ass may do her some good."

He let out the laugh he was holding. "Come on, beautiful. Let's get you out of here."

Chapter Twenty-One

I convinced Reid to let me drive to the private airport. I lied and told him driving helped me clear my mind. He agreed. I was going to let it go. I was going to get on the plane to Barbados and act as if my mother hadn't betrayed me worse than anyone else had, but I couldn't. I just could not. Instead of getting off on the correct exit, I bypassed it and headed back to my mother's house. Reid didn't say a word. He only shook his head.

"Are you sure you want to do this? This may get ugly?"

"I've never been so sure about anything in my life," I declared as I reached ninety on the highway.

"Why do women drive so damn fast?" Reid questioned as he tightened the slack on his seatbelt.

"Cause we've got shit to do. Just sit back and relax. I'm going to get us there safe and sound. Jesus knows my heart, and He wouldn't take me before I say what I need to say to her. He loves me and wouldn't disappoint me like that."

"I'm glad you have so much faith," he said as I pulled into the driveway. "Reid, you can just stay here until I come back. I promise you I don't need you to intervene. I've got this."

"Oh, I believe you. Holler if you need me and I'll be right there."

Sliding out the car, I trekked to the door, ringing the doorbell repeatedly until it swung open.

"Why are you back here? I told you I would call you. Just go home, Nuri," she demanded.

Her eyes flicked over me quickly...clocking my clothes, posture, expression. She was cataloging damage before emotion.

I stepped past her without asking permission. The look on her face changed.

"Little girl, are you trying to get slapped again?" she taunted.

I turned to face her fully. "How long?"

She blinked. "How long what?"

I pulled out my phone and held it to her face. Within an instant, her beautiful chocolate skin turned a pale grey. It wasn't guilt, it wasn't shame. It was fear.

"Where in the fuck did you get that, Nuri?" she asked sharply.

"How long," I repeated. "How long were you fucking Mercury, but an even better question—how long were you fucking my husband?"

She didn't answer right away. She straightened instead, lifting her chin like the question itself had offended her.

"What does it matter? You weren't fucking him. Someone had to, and as far as Mercury goes, I'm still fucking him. What does it matter to you? It doesn't mean shit to me. It's an arrangement we have going on."

Then she exhaled slowly and turned away, walking toward the kitchen like she expected me to follow.

"I understand you're upset about Jahi, and you have every right to be, but baby, he wasn't shit. Not only was he not shit, but he is dead, so let's not even worry about that. Besides, he was community dick at KPC. Just about every female with a fat ass that works there had dealings with him. This I know for certain. I even caught him one time."

"And instead of telling me about his indiscretions like a good mother would do, you decided to become one. How rich is that? You are a real piece of work."

"Whatever you say, Nuri. And Mercury...I don't see how me sleeping with Mercury is your concern."

"You are nuts, you know that? You think Mercury gives a fuck about you? He's the one that sent the pictures," I quipped. "Of you."

She stopped walking. Slowly, she turned back around.

"That man had no right—"

"—to what?" I interrupted. "To show me exactly who my mother really is? How could you do me like that? How could you do Dad like that? You don't care about anyone but yourself."

She crossed her arms. "Mercury and I are consenting adults. What we do in our spare time is our business."

"You are nothing but leverage," I said flatly. "And you didn't even realize it."

Her composure cracked just enough to show something frantic underneath.

"He would never—"

"He already has," I snapped. "He threatened me with you. With your body. With your reputation, and your old ass really thought that man gave a fuck about you."

She sat on a barstool like her legs were about to give out. I almost felt sorry for her. Almost.

"Nuri, you don't understand," she said quietly. "Everything I've built..."

"I know exactly what you've built. You've built an image so fragile it can be destroyed by a simple photograph."

"Don't talk to your mother that way."

"Oh, now you want to remember you're my mother. Did that cross your mind when Jahi's dick was sliding past your cheeks? Did it?" I yelled.

"Ssshhhhhhh. Keep your voice down before your father or the help hears you."

Standing up and walking to me, she stopped inches from my face. Staring me down and breathing hard. Finally, she dropped her arms.

"What do you want?" she asked coldly.

I stepped closer. "First, I'm going to check on my father. Then immediately after, I want you to stay the fuck out of my life. Forever. You are dead to me. Can you do that, you lowly bitch? And I dare you to touch me again. I swear to God, I will wipe the floor with your whore ass."

Her face crumpled then, not dramatic or performative like normal, but quietly. Like a woman finally realizing the relationship she destroyed would never be repaired.

She gestured toward the back room where my father was.

"He's my father. I don't need a supervised visit. I would like some time alone with him."

She didn't say a word as I sashayed past her on the way to his room. Instead, she shook her head and went the other way. I entered the room and closed the door behind me. He was perched up in the middle of the bed watching Judge Mathis.

"Hey, Daddy. How are you feeling? I was told you had an incident."

"Oh baby, that wasn't nothing. Every now and again, if

my blood pressure gets a little too high, I feel a little weak. That's all it was."

"Are you sure, Daddy?" I asked, side-eyeing him in the process.

"Yes, I'm sure. Why? Did you hear something else?"

"No, I wasn't sure what happened. I tried to call, but Mom wouldn't tell me anything as usual. That's why I'm here."

"Well, I appreciate you coming to check on your old man. Enough about me. How have you been doing, baby? I've been calling you off and on and leaving messages. I know you're going through a lot right now. Losing a spouse has to be very difficult. Your mother has her moments, but I don't know what I'd do without her."

My heart ached for him. Refusing to let it show, I answered his question.

"I'm doing as well as can be expected. It's all so overwhelming, but I manage. Considering that they have no idea if it was an accident or if someone else caused the crash...I've taken on a security detail."

"Baby, do you really think someone really did that to your husband? I know he was a little slick at the mouth and cocky, but I can't imagine anyone hurting him that way."

"Daddy, I think you give people too much credit. You've always seen the good in people even when it's not there. There are some terrible people in this world. People that will step over you and do whatever they can to save themselves. You are married to one."

"Oh, give your mama a little grace. She loves you, baby. She just doesn't know how to show it all the time."

"If you say so, Daddy. Anyhow, I just came to check on you. Now I see you are fine, and I can rest easy tonight. I've been worried sick since I found out. Oh, and I didn't tell Mom, but I'm going to tell you. When I leave here, I am headed to our...well, my home in Barbados. I need some alone time."

"Baby, if that is what you need to do to heal, then you do just that." He leaned over and kissed me on the cheek. "All I ask is that you give your old man a call when you arrive and you check in with me from time to time. I need to know my little girl is okay. Can you do that for me?"

"Of course I can. I love you, and I'll see you when I get back."

With those words to my father, I sauntered past my mother and back out to my car where Reid was waiting patiently.

"Are we good now? Did you get it all out your system?" he questioned as he placed his phone in his lap.

Nodding yes, "I think so. I feel better than I have in a long time. Now, to the airport for real this time, and you can get back in the driver's side. I hate driving," I admitted.

"I don't know what I was thinking firing everybody after Jahi died. The maid, the drivers...hell, everybody. I regret that shit now."

"I guess it's lucky for me that you were in the hiring mood for a moment," he said as he sat back in the driver's seat.

"When I think about it, Reid, you've been in my life for longer than I've known. That doesn't seem fair. Especially now, getting to know you, Jahi and I could have benefited greatly from a friend like you. You're straightforward and on the side of right. That's what he needed."

"Unfortunately, I was hired to do a job. Yes, we were friends, but I don't believe he would have taken my advice when it came to you or dealings with the company. He was too damn stubborn for that. By the time I came back into his life, he'd gotten used to people doing whatever he asked. I just did what I was paid to do."

"Yeah, you're right. It was too little, too late," I whispered to myself as we backed out of the driveway. As we traveled up the road, I entered the address to the private airport that Jahi always used and placed a call to Paige to check on Maya's condition.

I hesitated a second before pressing the send button.

"Girl," Paige answered on the first ring, her voice still tight. "I was just about to call you."

"How is she?" I asked quietly.

"She's stable. They said she's lucky that whoever did this didn't finish what they started."

My stomach flipped. "Lucky," I repeated. "She is blessed, not lucky."

The phone went silent.

"Don't do that, Nuri," Paige warned softly.

"Do what?"

"That thing where you start blaming yourself again."

I didn't answer because she wasn't wrong. I was indeed blaming myself.

"I should have warned you all. I also should have seen something like this coming."

"Nuri," she barked. "Stop. This is not on you."

"But it feels like it is."

Silence stretched between us again. Then I exhaled slowly.

"I'm leaving."

Paige didn't respond right away.

"Leaving and going where?" she asked.

"To one of my favorite places in the entire world. Barbados."

"You're joking, right? Our friend is laying up in the hospital hurt and you're about to go on vacation?" she scoffed.

"I wouldn't exactly call it a vacation, Paige. It's too

much going on. I need to get away for a bit. Maybe all this bullshit will die down if I just leave."

"Since when do you run?"

"I'm not running," I said quickly, though the words didn't feel true. "I just need...space. I need air. I need to think."

"You think Mercury's just going to pause his bullshit because you got on your jet and left?"

I swallowed before answering. "Mercury and I had a conversation. I convinced him that I'm not a problem. That I don't know anything. He said he would leave me alone. Hopefully, this is true and we can all go back to our regularly scheduled program."

Paige sighed, and I heard Charity's voice in the background asking what was going on.

"She feels responsible," Paige told her.

I closed my eyes.

"Put her on speaker." A second later, Charity's voice filled the line. "Nuri," she said gently. "You are not God. You didn't orchestrate this. And you don't get to punish yourself for someone else's evil."

"I know," I whispered.

"No, you don't, because if you did, you wouldn't be talking about disappearing to Barbados like this is some kind of romantic exile."

I almost smiled despite the way I was feeling.

"I'm just saying, I'll be gone for a while. I wanted you to know before you heard it from someone else."

Paige came back on the line.

"So, you're really just going to vanish?"

"Only for a little while. I need to breathe without feeling like every shadow is my fault."

Paige's voice softened. "Just don't disappear on us, and your ass better call us every day."

"I will. I promise."

"Alright," Paige muttered. "Keep us posted and call me if you even think of doing something reckless."

"Will do. I love y'all."

We hung up.

"This is the perfect time to back out. We could go back to your house. Straighten up, get things in order, and I can whip us up a nice dinner." Reid said as he bumped my shoulder.

"Keep driving," I spat. "Fuck that house. It'll be here when we get back, and so will the mess left inside."

We traveled for another twenty minutes before reaching the airport. The jet was waiting. It was stark white and sleek. Just the way I remembered it looking. As we boarded, the cabin lights glowed warm and soft. The air smelled faintly of leather and mahogany. Reid moved through the space, checking every corner, every door, and detail. Just as he did at the house.

When the plane lifted into the sky, I felt something lift with it. The jet leveled off somewhere over the Atlantic Ocean. Reid loosened his tie and leaned back. He rolled his shoulders like he carried more weight than just a gun and a job title. I watched him from the corner of my eye. He was slightly less guarded once the plane steadied. Once the doors were sealed and there was nowhere else he needed to be. No one to protect. Just me.

"You okay?" he asked, noticing me staring into the cabin ceiling.

"I was just thinking about your house."

His brow lifted. "What about it?"

"It's beautiful," I said slowly, choosing my words carefully. "It's grand, but not cold. It felt lived in. Loved. I didn't expect that."

He exhaled through his nose. "Most people don't."

"I guess I didn't picture private gates, nurses, and acreage. I didn't realize security paid like that."

He turned toward me then, studying my face.

"There's money in it if you're good. If you survive long enough."

"Looks like you're doing more than surviving."

He didn't respond right away.

After inhaling sharply, he said, "I bought that house years ago. Back when my mother was still working double shifts and refusing to sit down. I'd asked her time and time again to move to Atlanta so we could be closer, and each time she said no. That she loved her little shotgun house that had been passed down from my Meemaw in Algiers. So I let it go."

He stared out the window, the darkness reflecting back at him.

"She was a nurse...well, still is. Deep down in her bones. She took care of everyone," he continued. "Neighbors, family, patients, and strangers. If you were hurting, she made room for you. She always said God didn't give her the gift of healing to keep it to herself."

His voice trembled a tad.

"When she got sick...it was quiet. I mean really quiet. People started disappearing. People stopped calling, and all of a sudden, everyone had lives they needed to get back to."

The more he talked, the more my chest ached for him.

"ALS doesn't wait for anyone. One day she was strong enough to lift grown men out of a hospital bed. The next, she couldn't lace her shoes. So, I quit everything. There was no debating or hesitation. I moved her into my house, took over her care, and hired the best nurses I could find to care for her when I couldn't be there. I learned how to do things I'd never thought I'd have to do for the woman who raised me."

He finally looked at me again.

"That was the least I could do for all the sacrifices she

made. For every dream she put on hold so I could chase mine."

My eyes started to burn.

"That's why you are like this," I said quietly. "Why you don't half-step?"

He gave a small, knowing smile. "When life shows you what really matters, everything else feels optional."

"What about your father?"

His expression barely changed.

"I really don't know him. He left early. Left my mother with more responsibility than help. That's about all I've got on him."

I nodded, sensing the line and making sure not to cross it. We sat in silence for a moment. Silence that didn't need to be filled. We'd reached that level of comfortability with each other. Then my gaze drifted back to the image of his home—the sweeping drive, the stone, the care he put into every detail.

"You've done well for yourself. Better than well."

He shrugged. "It didn't come easy. Everything I have, I built."

"That's what I mean," I replied. "Brick by brick. You ever think about expanding your business? Partnering? I have capital. I could be a silent investor."

He turned fully toward me and shook his head. "No."

I blinked. "You didn't even let me finish."

“I don’t need to,” he said calmly. “I appreciate the thought, but I don’t take investors.”

“Why not? I’m genuinely curious.”

“Because it’s mine. I built my company from nothing. Slept in my car and hotels in between contracts. Took the jobs nobody wanted. I made mistakes...paid for them and learned how to do better. I don’t owe anyone a percentage of that.”

“So it’s pride?”

“It’s principle,” he corrected. “I do just fine without anyone’s money.”

There was something attractive about that. He wasn’t flashy, and his demeanor wasn’t an act. He was a solid dude on his grown man shit, and I loved it.

“Duly noted,” I chirped. “I’ll stop trying to buy you.”

He flashed a huge smile my way. “Appreciated.”

The plane continued its steady path forward, carrying us somewhere new, somewhere temporary, somewhere that might feel like the relief I so desperately needed. I leaned back in my seat, eyes drifting closed. And for a brief moment...I felt free.

As the plane began its descent hours later, the lights of Barbados shimmered beneath us. For a moment, everything felt peaceful. Too peaceful. As soon as the wheels touched the runway, my phone vibrated. Once. Then twice. It was an unknown number again.

Reid shook his head no. "Don't answer. Whatever or whoever it is can wait. You have to put yourself in a different space mentally. You can't do that if you are still feeding what you left."

"That's great advice, Reid, but what if it's Paige or Charity with an update about Maya? What if something happened to her?"

"Go ahead, but promise me...after this, you will put it on DND."

"Got it," I answered.

"Enjoy your little vacation, Mrs. Laurent."

"Wait, how did you—"

"I've got eyes everywhere, and I need you to understand that. I also need you to know, when they made one jet, they made two. Jahi and I would fly out sometimes from the same airport. You must forget. I know everyone in Atlanta. Most of them are in my pocket one way or the other, so tread lightly. Enjoy."

My fingers tightened around the phone. He hung up, and suddenly I didn't feel free at all anymore.

Chapter Twenty-Two

By the time my heels touched Barbadian soil, fear was the first thing to greet me. It clung to me the way humidity clung to skin in the south. Mercury's voice still echoed in my ears, each word calculated. For a moment, I felt dumb for thinking distance could make all my worries go away. But Barbados didn't feel like danger. It felt like letting out a breath I'd been holding for too long.

The house sat on a cliff overlooking the sea. It boasted all white stone and wide glass windows. It was wrapped in bougainvillea, and the air smelled of salt. The house wasn't loud and flashy like my Atlanta home. It was...peaceful.

And peace was foreign at this point.

Walking ahead of me, Reid scanned the perimeter. His presence was steady and grounded. He didn't speak much as we entered the house, just checked doors, windows, and the cameras. It was his version of prayer.

When he finally turned to me, his expression softened.

"You're safe here," he said.

I didn't argue because I knew I would be.

By the next morning, Barbados had worked its way into my psyche. The sun poured through the windows like honey. The ocean talked in the distance. I stood barefoot on the terrace with my coffee in hand, watching the waves roll in.

"You look like you're finally remembering how to breathe and exhale. I'm happy to see it," Reid said behind me.

I smiled faintly. "Good morning, and you are correct. I'm remembering how to breathe. One second at a time. Honestly, I forgot what quiet felt like."

He stepped beside me, not too close, not too far.

"We should go into town and blend in a little."

"Is that allowed?" I teased.

"Don't get used to it," he smirked.

The town was alive. Colors everywhere. Brightly painted buildings, bright dresses, fresh fruit stands stocked with mangoes and guavas. Music spilled out of every doorway, and laughter floated through the air like perfume. For the first time since Jahi died, people weren't looking at me with pity or curiosity. They didn't know my story, and I didn't have to tell them.

We walked through the market slowly. Reid was close but not hovering. His presence was feeling more of a companion than a guard. Vendors called out to us, offering fried fish, coconut bread, flying fish cutters, and rum punch.

"You have to try this," I said, handing him a paper plate piled high with food.

He looked at it suspiciously. "I don't eat everyone's cooking," he whispered.

"Boy, take this damn plate and grub. I promise you won't regret it."

"You trust random street food more than I do," he said.

"You trust strangers with guns," I replied. "This is simply fish. Now eat the damn food."

He sighed and took a bite. His eyes widened slightly. I laughed.

"Don't act surprised," I said. "You've been missing out on life. The shit is bussing, isn't it?"

He stared at me for a moment, like he was trying to decide whether he wanted to argue.

Instead, he said, "I love to see you enjoying yourself, Nuri. I don't think I've ever seen you smile this much. It's so beautiful."

I nodded. I hadn't smiled this much in a long time. I was genuinely happy, until I wasn't.

We were walking past a small café when I saw him. At first, I thought my mind was playing tricks on me. The man stood across the street, half turned, sunlight catching the side of his face. Tall, familiar posture. The same careless tilt of the head.

My heart slammed.

"Reid," I whispered.

He stopped instantly.

"What is it? What's wrong?"

I stared across the street. The man turned, and for a split second, I saw him clearly. Jahi. Alive. My breath left my body like it had been stolen.

"Did you see that?" I asked, my voice trembling.

Reid followed my eyes. The man was gone.

"See what?" he asked, looking around.

"I swear I just saw him," I said. "Jahi. I swear he was right there. He was standing right there."

Reid looked at me carefully.

"Nuri," he said gently. "Jahi is dead. We saw his body. We saw him lowered into the ground. He's gone, sweetheart."

"Don't talk to me like I'm nuts. I know how it sounds, but I know what I saw," I said quickly. "I know he's dead, but I saw him. Or at least someone that looks like him."

"You know they say we all have a doppelganger. Maybe his is from Barbados. Anyway, I'm going to grab some of this delicious fresh food to cook for dinner tonight. Is there anything you'd like to eat in particular?"

Still shook from what I saw, it took a moment for me to register what Reid had asked me.

"I'm so sorry, Reid. What were you saying?"

"I asked if there was anything in particular you wanted to eat tonight?"

"No, nothing in particular. As long as it's good," I murmured as I continued looking around for the man.

As Reid shopped for food, he spoke to the vendors like he belonged there, like he'd done this before. He picked things out with care...fresh fish wrapped in paper, herbs he or I couldn't name, freshly baked bread still warm enough to steam through the bag. He listened when they talked, he smiled when they joked, and he paid without haggling. Reid knew respect mattered more than the price.

Then we walked around purchasing clothing to replace the ones we didn't pack. When I pulled out my credit card, Reid looked insulted.

"Umm, what are you doing?" he asked.

"I'm getting ready to pay for everything. This was my trip, so I should front all costs."

"Yes, ma'am, I'm aware, but you can put that back up.

I've got it. I wouldn't feel comfortable allowing you to buy my clothes."

"But you're about to pay for mine, Reid. Make it make sense. How is it okay for you to buy my things but not the other way around?" I questioned.

Sucking his teeth, he muttered, "Please don't make me show out in front of these good Barbadian people. You're not paying, and that's final," he said as he shoved money into the shop owner's hand.

I smiled and walked away a little, watching him like that did something to me.

Back at the house, the kitchen filled with the sounds of the knife raking against the cutting board, oil popping in a pan, and music low but present. It was a whole vibe. For a minute, I forgot why we were here. I forgot about Mercury. Forgot about blood, hospitals, and threats that came through phones instead of doors.

We ate outside, the sky darkening above us. The food seemed to ground us. It was simple. Everything felt good. It felt honest. Although I didn't say much, I couldn't stop thinking about what I'd seen, or what I thought I saw.

Jahi.

I couldn't get the image out of my head.

After dinner, Reid leaned back in his chair halfway and truly relaxed. His shoulders loosened, and the sharpness finally left his eyes.

"You good?" I teased.

"Yeah, good and tired."

He didn't make it far after that. Going back inside, he fell asleep on the couch, his body falling victim to the quiet and peace. With one arm slung over his chest, his jaw relaxed, and he was out.

I covered him with a throw and told myself not to stare. He was beautiful. There was no other way to put it. This man was it. Mind, body, and soul.

Then the house started talking. At first, it was nothing obvious. A feeling more than anything. The kind you get when something around you feels unfamiliar. Nothing jumped out at me, but it was like something had been moved...disturbed. As I walked barefoot through the hallways, I opened the doors slowly. After the doors, the drawers were next.

That's when I saw it...clothes that weren't mine. They were worn with no tags, and some were folded. Then a man's shirt jumped out at me. Jahi had a certain style, and none of the things in the drawer seemed familiar. Reid had put some of the things we purchased at the market in the drawers, but as far as I knew...those were in the other room. Not the master bedroom.

Then the worst. A cute little romper that I'd never wear. It was four sizes too small for me. There was no way an ass my size would have fit. Last but not least, there were sandals under the bed that weren't my size.

A lump formed in my throat. The more I looked, the more I discovered. A toothbrush that didn't belong to me. A half-used bottle of perfume tucked under the sink. Lip gloss in a drawer I'd never used before.

There I stood, shaking, with my hands braced on the counter.

He brought them here. To my house. The one I picked out and decorated. Every square inch of this house had my touch and my touch alone in it. And to think...while I was flying in and out of cities, hosting events, smiling for cameras, pretending we were still something we hadn't been in years—he was here. With them. In this house. Letting them sleep in sheets that were never meant for anyone but us.

It was clear. I didn't know this man. I hadn't known him for a long time.

I felt stupid all over again. I grew angrier in a way that made my head throb. The papers came last. They were tucked where someone thought I wouldn't look. Business documents just like the ones back at the safe. Transactions that didn't align. Names I recognized and others I didn't. Accounts layered under accounts. Dates that overlapped with anniversaries, with trips, and nights he told me he was working late.

Things that made me know his life had been running parallel to mine...never intersecting the way I thought it did. Incriminating wasn't even the right word. The clothing, the toiletries, the documents were revelatory.

I sat on the floor with papers spread around me like evidence. A woman surrounded by proof that love hadn't just slipped through her fingers; it had been replaced.

Replaced by secrets and greed. By the choices he made while looking at me in the face and telling me we were good...that everything was fine.

Somewhere behind me, the house creaked. I gathered the papers slowly and carefully and placed them back where I found them. Once again, my dead husband had let me down. How many times could a dead man tell me I wasn't enough? That he didn't love me?

I wasn't sure, but if I had anything to do with it...it would be the last time.

Chapter Twenty-Three

I woke up before the sun. The birds hadn't even started chirping yet. The house was quiet, and Reid was still asleep on the couch where I'd left him. He had one arm thrown over his eyes like he was blocking out the sun that hadn't risen yet. He looked younger like that. Less rigid. Less like the man who carried my safety on his shoulders.

I told myself I was stepping out for air.

I told myself a lot of things.

I walked with no real destination, letting my thoughts drag behind me like rope that tied me to the past. The town was quieter in the early morning, but not empty. A few shop owners were lifting gates. Some were sweeping their stoops. I found one with an open door and trekked inside to see if they were serving coffee. A good cup of joe was needed.

That's when I saw him.

Not a glimpse this time. Not a trick of light or a shadow passing too fast to name.

Him.

Standing near a fruit stand, laughing at something the vendor said, head still tilted like I remembered. My heart stuttered. He looked so much like Jahi it felt violent. He had the same height and build; he carried himself like the world would bend in his direction if he commanded. Just like Jahi. Even the way his mouth curved when he grinned...it was wrong how right it was.

The only physical difference I noticed was he had a birthmark on the side of his neck. Jahi did not.

I stood there too long. Long enough to be sure that grief wasn't playing a cruel trick on me. This man could have been my husband's reflection if the mirror had decided to lie. My hands shook as I pulled my phone out. I just dialed.

"Hello?" his mother answered, her voice already tight because of the time.

"I'm so sorry for calling this time of morning, Mom, but I—I need to tell you something. I saw someone just now. Someone who looks just like Jahi. Not similar, but identical. It was uncanny."

Silence.

Then, "Nuri, listen to me. You're tired, sweetheart, and it's early. You've been through a lot. My son is dead, and trust me, there was no one like Jahi. No one," she barked.

"I know, but I'm telling you. I know what I saw."

"Well, you didn't," she snapped. Then she softened just as fast. "I mean, you didn't see him. You need to stop looking for ghosts, baby. Like I said, my son is dead. Now, I'm tired, dear. We will talk later."

The line went dead before I could respond.

I stood there staring at my phone. The slight buzz of the town creeping back into my ears.

Why did she sound like that? Why did she rush me off the phone like I'd said something dangerous?

I fought with that question in my mind for at least three minutes before exhaustion won. I pushed the thought aside and headed back to the house.

Walking into the house, the smell hit me first. Butter, coffee, and something frying. Reid stood at the stove like he belonged there, shirtless with bed head, but he still moved with a confidence that made my pussy slick.

"You know," he said without turning around, "most people wake their security detail before wandering off into foreign towns."

I smiled, walked over to him, and cupped his chin.

"You were sleeping so peacefully. I didn't want to disturb you."

"Me sleeping wasn't permission for you to run off without me. Next time, just wake me up."

"Will do. Now, what are you over there cooking?"

"Food."

"What kind of food?"

"Good food," he responded with that knowing smirk.

"Well, while you were in here cooking good food, I saw Jahi's doppelgänger again. I'm telling you. That man is his spitting image. I should have taken a picture. Then she would have believed me."

Reid raised his head. "She, as in who?"

"His mother. I called her to tell her that her son has a twin, and she acted like I was crazy. Like there was no way someone could look like him. It was honestly weird because she snapped on me a little. I know it's early, but I didn't deserve being talked to like a nutso."

"Nuri, it's probably hard for her to hear things like that. She probably misses him more than you could imagine. After all, there is nothing like a mother's love."

"Well, as you know, I don't know anything about that."

"I'm sorry. I didn't mean to sound insensitive. We don't need to talk about this anyway. Not with all this good food over here waiting to be devoured."

"Oh, my feelings aren't hurt. It takes a lot more than bringing up good parents to hurt my feelings. I actually want to talk about it because I would like to know what you think?"

"Honestly, Nuri, I think his mother is grieving, and she doesn't want any reminders of the pain, the hurt. That's all. Tell me, what kind of parents were they to Jahi?"

"Oh man, they were the best. To him and me. They were proud and super supportive of anything he was interested in doing. I used to tease him and tell him God gave us the wrong parents. I should have been with them and he with my parents. There was no need for that though. From the moment he introduced me to them, they showed me nothing but the warmest love."

"They sound like good people," Reid said while smacking on his fishcake.

I continued, "They are. We had a completely different upbringing. You see, Jahi came from humble beginnings. He went to school on scholarship, and what the scholarship didn't cover, his parents did. From my understanding, they worked extremely hard to get their baby boy off to college. Both of his parents held two jobs for most of his life. He told me that from an early age they told him he had to be better than them."

Reid nodded. "I believe that is what all parents want from their kids. To grow up and do better than they did."

"Well, he did. He loved and thanked them all the time for pushing him to become better. As soon as money started rolling in, he paid off their house, bought them both brand new Cadillacs and a monthly stipend. They acted like the sun rose and set on him. Every time we would go back to Cleveland to visit, they would call all the family members over just so they could brag on him, and I hated it because he ate that shit up. He would leave feeling ten feet tall."

"Yeah, man. Back in college, he always spoke about wanting to take care of his parents. He knew back then he'd be somebody. We all did."

"Well, enough of talking about my dearly departed husband. Are you ready for some fun?" I grabbed his hands and pulled him up from the table. "We are going dancing," I muttered while winding my hips.

"The hell we are, Nuri. Look at me. I'm 6'4. Do you know how crazy I would look out there trying to cut a rug? Island people take dancing very seriously. I don't want to insult anyone with my stiffness."

Shit, I could think of one stiff thing I'd like to take seriously. Pulling my mind from the gutter, I tried to ease his mind. "Boy, please. Island people only get insulted when you don't join in. They hate to see people standing around holding up the wall. They want you to enjoy their music, their culture. Come on, Reid. Please," I begged.

"Okay, but don't expect too much. I wouldn't want you to be disappointed."

He got up, grabbed the plates, and padded back into the kitchen. I walked up behind him without thinking, without planning, without stopping myself the way I usually do. Maybe it was the intoxicating smell of food. Maybe it was the way he moved so easily in my space, like he belonged there. Or maybe it was the simple fact that I felt safe for the first time in a long time.

My lips brushed his before my mind could catch up. It was like instinct. The second it registered, I pulled back.

"I'm sorry," I said quickly. "I shouldn't have—"

Shaking his head, he turned toward me. It wasn't anger, judgment, or irritation on his face, but restraint. The kind that came with years of practice.

"Nuri, don't forget who I am, what I told you, and why I'm here."

The words landed heavier than he probably intended because I hadn't forgotten. I'd just stopped separating things. And when I looked at him standing there, close enough to feel, yet distant enough to hurt, I realized how thin that line had become.

The festival should have been noise and distraction, but it turned into something else entirely. Music wrapped around us, bass vibrating through my bones, the crowd pressing in, rum loosening what fear had clenched tight. Reid laughed more than I'd seen him laugh before. I caught him watching me when he thought I wasn't paying attention. His eyes were softer, warmer and sparkled with sexiness.

We danced, not close at first. Then closer than we should have. By the time we made it back to the house, the air between us felt heavy. Entering the house, I went to my bedroom, and he went to the other.

I lay awake. My body still vibrating with adrenaline. Without thinking, I disrobed and climbed back into the bed. My skin prickled with heat as I licked my fingers and slid them down to my clit. I thought about the way Reid's hips moved as we danced. The way his arms flexed as he twirled me around. How beautiful he was when his inhibitions were down.

I started slowly but quickly picked up the pace. My body wanted...needed this. Without warning, Reid's name found its way into my moans.

Before I could realize what I'd said, Reid was already standing in the doorway.

We didn't talk, we didn't negotiate, we just...stopped pretending we didn't want each other. He threw the covers back and marveled over my body before sliding in next to me. I flipped around toward him and took his tongue into my mouth. The taste of rum punch still lingered on his lips.

"Nuri," he whispered. "This isn't...simple."

"Nothing about us has been," I replied.

That was all it took. My hands slid down to his member slowly, giving him every chance to pull away. When he didn't, I leaned into the touch instead. Something in him snapped, not violently or recklessly, but like he was done holding himself together.

He kissed me like he knew exactly where his mouth wanted to be. I melted into him, my body remembering things my heart had been starved of. My heart raced as I stroked his member, feeling his heartbeat thump against my hands.

I slid down and took him into my mouth. His head rolled back as he winced from the pleasure.

"I shouldn't want you this bad, Reid," my voice breaking.

His jaw flexed. "Neither should I, but please don't stop. Please."

I continued sucking him, his hands firmly entangled in my hair. I relaxed my jaw and deep-throated as much of him as I could. His dick definitely matched his body frame and stature. I breathed him in, enjoying his scent and the taste of his skin.

Slowly, he started fucking my face and picked up the

pace as he drew near. Me being the edging queen wasn't about to let him get away that easy. Without notice, I came up for air. He looked down at me like I'd committed a federal offense.

"I want to feel your tongue. I want you to suck my pussy until I beg you to stop."

Pulling me up, he flipped me over and slid down to my center. Cupping my ass in the palms of his hands, he dove in. He relentlessly lapped at my clit, sucking every drop of nectar he could.

"Shit, Reid. Hold on...hold on. I'm not ready to cum just yet. Wait, pleaaaaaaase."

It was over. Before I could finish my sentence, I came so hard it felt like my body went into shock. Without warning, he slid deep into my yoni, filling me up beyond capacity. He was so deep that my cervix was quaking. Slow strokes at first, and I savored every moment. The sensation felt unreal to me.

"This is what you wanted, Nuri. Isn't it? Tell me, is this what you wanted?" he muttered as he fucked through the moans.

His strokes were powerful. Masterful and laced with so much passion. His hands and tongue roamed parts of my body that hadn't been touched in ages. It was giving sensory overload, and I loved every second of it. Over and over, he pounded my pussy until I begged for a break.

"Please, Reid. Please...it's too much. Can we—" I muttered as my eyes rolled into the back of my head.

"No. Whatever you're about to ask, the answer is no. You are going to take this dick until I cum as hard as you did, and baby, that could take some time."

He never broke his stride. He continued thrusting, eventually filling me with his love. Reid proved he was a walking, talking weapon in every sense of the word.

When we finally stopped, I rested my head on his chest, listening to his heart race. He didn't pull away from me, but I could feel the war in him.

"I told God I'd wait," he murmured. "And now here you are."

I swallowed hard. "Yes, you did, and now here I am. Don't do that, Reid. Don't be angry at yourself. You told Him you would wait for the right one. Who says I'm not her?"

He closed his eyes and exhaled.

Chapter Twenty-Four

In my sleep, I faintly heard the sound of metal turning when I should not have been. I thought I was dreaming. My mind tried to soften it, half sleep excuses, but my body knew better. Apparently, so did Reid because he was already moving. One second, he was beside me, warm and solid, the next he was off the bed and moving towards the door.

"Stay," he whispered, and for once, I did exactly what I was told.

The lock unturned and the door opened. I barely had time to sit up before Reid raised the gun.

"Reid—" My heart catapulted out of my chest.

"WHOA... WAIT. DON'T. PLEASE. DON'T SHOOT ME."

His voice cracked mid plea. He was panicked but very much alive. I leaned forward just enough to see his face, and my breath left my body. It was like the universe had played a cruel trick. Like someone had taken Jahi's face, shifted it just enough to feel wrong, and dropped it in my lap like a missile.

"Oh, my God," I breathed.

The man froze, hands halfway up, keys dangling from his fingers.

Reid's voice was steady but lethal. "Why does he look like—"

"Jahi," I finished faintly.

"Who the hell are you, and why do you have a key to this house?"

The man swallowed hard. "Because I live here."

"That's the wrong answer," Reid said.

I stood, legs still weak from last night, and locked eyes on this man. Jahi's face. Not similar, not close, but identical. Same mouth, same eyes, same sharp line of the jaw I'd kissed a thousand times. The same face that haunted me in sleep and memories of paperwork and unanswered questions.

"I saw you yesterday in town and then again this morning," I admitted.

His mouth tilted. "Well, you're looking at me now like you've just seen a ghost."

"It's because it's like I'm looking at one. You look exactly like him," I chirped.

He sighed, rubbing his face. "Umm, if you are speaking of Jahi, then you are correct. I look like him because I'm his twin."

Reid sucked his teeth. "Of course you are, because why wouldn't you be. Damn, Nuri. Jahi sure knows how to keep a brother on his toes."

We ended up at the kitchen table, the three of us sitting like strangers forced into the same dream. Reid finally lowered the gun, but I could feel his attention circling us like a guard dog.

"My name is Noah," the man said. "And no, he didn't tell anyone about me. He wanted me better before we crossed that bridge, and I'm now better than better. We were supposed to be heading back to the States this month to surprise his family. They never told him he was adopted. He found that out when he found me."

I shook my head in disbelief once again.

"Jahi and I were adopted out to different families," Noah continued. "I guess our biological parents couldn't afford two babies at that time, so they gave us up, and in the process, we were split up. Jahi went to a good family. One that loved him and cared for him like they'd given birth to him. Mine... not so much, but that's another story for another day."

The words landed heavy and familiar in a way I didn't like.

"I bounced around for a while... foster care, bad decisions, and worse people," he said with a shrug that failed to mask how he really felt. "The last ten years of my life had been rough. I was homeless, strung out, and sleeping under an L train in Chicago. I was just about ready to end it all."

My chest tightened.

"He found me two years ago," Noah said. "An ancestry test. It turns out identical twins don't hide well from the internet."

I pressed my fingers to my lips as I stared at him. I couldn't believe what I was hearing or seeing, but stranger things have happened, so I listened.

"He cleaned me up, then dragged my ass to rehab," Noah said. "Then he brought me here. Paid for treatment and told me I could stay here in this house as long as I was sober."

Reid frowned. "This house?"

"Yes," Noah nodded. "This house. He bought this house for his wife."

Reid and I stared at one another.

Noah continued, "He told me he'd warn me if she ever came so I could clear out. You know, make the place look normal."

My head spun. "Well, where have you been the past few days?"

"At my girlfriend's. Now, I have a few questions myself. Who are you all, and if you know my brother, then where is he? I've been calling him for months now. He often checks on me but it's been crickets."

"Noah, I am his wife. My name is Nuri, and it's nice to meet you."

"Wait, if you are his wife, then why are you in the bed with this man?"

He stood up from the table, offended as if he was Jahi himself.

"Please sit down and listen. I promise I will get around to all that, but I need to tell you something."

He sat back down and then looked up. Something in my face must have warned him. He began to look nervous.

"What is it?"

I stood, walked around the table, and took his hand.

"Jahi passed away about three months ago. He died in a car accident. I'm so sorry to have to tell you this."

Noah let out a sound I'd never heard before. He folded forward, crying so hard his body was visibly shaking.

"No, no. No. Why? Why?" he cried.

I dropped to my knees beside him, arms wrapping around his shaking body, trying to hold him together.

"He saved me," Noah cried. "I didn't even get the

chance to thank him. To show him how much I appreciated him for doing all he did for me. This is so fucked up."

Between sobs, Noah let out a broken laugh. "He got me clean. Gave me a life, and now... just like that, he's gone. This is how my luck is. This is how it's always gone for me."

I held him while he fell apart. Tears began sliding down my own face. For a moment, he lay nestled in my bosom as Reid looked on with sympathy. I stayed on the floor with Noah until the worst of it passed.

Eventually, Noah wiped his face with the heel of his hand and looked up at me, eyes red and unfocused. His gaze slid past me to Reid, who was standing near the window now, arms folded, alert but deliberately removed from the moment.

Noah frowned. "Why are you here with him?"

The question wasn't accusatory. It was confused. Like he was still trying to ground himself in a reality that had shifted so many times in one morning.

I exhaled slowly, bracing myself. "It's... a lot."

Reid glanced at me. "I'll step outside, if—"

"No," I said quickly. "Stay. It's ok."

Noah noticed the way I said it. He also noticed the way Reid didn't argue.

Pulling my knees towards me, I grounded and readied myself to empty the truth like a clip.

"I hired Reid to protect me," I voiced. "After Jahi died, things around me didn't stop. Things started to escalate in a way that made me feel unsafe. Jahi had discovered things within the company he worked for. Things that a lot of people would like to remain undiscovered. This caused major issues. Someone started watching and threatening me after he died. They attacked one of my best friends and even broke into my house and ripped it to pieces looking for something."

Noah's expression darkened with every sentence.

"And then there were the messages," I continued. "Photos, information that shouldn't exist. Someone started using my husband's secrets like weapons."

Noah picked himself off the floor and sat in the chair. His brow furrowed, and his jaw was tight.

"So you're telling me someone was threatening my brother?" he said, disbelief laced with fury.

"Yes."

Noah stared at the floor, nodding his head slowly like he was putting pieces of a puzzle together.

"He told me," Noah said suddenly.

I looked at him. "Told you what?"

"That he'd messed up bad. That he was involved in shit he couldn't walk away from without someone ending up hurt. I didn't ask for details because every time I did, he'd simply say, 'I'll fix it. I just need time.'" He said if anything ever happened to him," Noah continued, voice rougher now, "it wouldn't be an accident. And that if people came sniffing around you, it meant he hadn't cleaned it up fast enough."

The room went cold.

Reid straightened. "Did he say who?"

Noah shook his head. "No names. Just the people he was dealing with didn't scare easily, and they would do anything they had to regain control if they lost it. I didn't know what all that meant. I just knew my brother was in trouble but thought he had everything under control. I guess he didn't. I know he was nervous about it all, though. He told me this house wasn't just a gift but a place of refuge. It was off the grid, clean and quiet. He said you thought he was eager to purchase it because you wanted it so bad, but that wasn't the only reason."

I let out a humorless laugh. "Shit, Noah, that's the story of my marriage."

With those words, Noah looked at me. Really looked at me, and the resemblance hurt in a new way now. It wasn't just physical, but emotional. Noah and Jahi carried the same stubborn loyalty. The same instinct and the same pride of carrying too much alone.

"I hate that I wasn't there," he said. "I hate he was fighting something and didn't tell me what losing could really cost."

"That was Jahi... he did shit on his own accord. No permission. No instructions," I quipped.

Reid's voice was steady but edged. "Noah, whatever he was involved in...it's not finished."

Noah nodded slowly. "Then we have a problem."

My stomach twisted. "What kind?"

"The kind," Noah said, eyes lifting to mine, "where someone thought my brother dying would end things."

He shook his head once. "And they're about to find out thats not the case."

Chapter Twenty-Five

I realized Noah wasn't grieving the way I thought the moment we landed in Atlanta. Grief usually folds you inward. It makes you soft in places you didn't know you could be. It makes the world feel too loud, too bright, and too alive for what you're dealing with.

Noah did the opposite. He went still. Not numb. Not detached. Just... still. Like every movement and breath was being clocked. He didn't ask questions out loud. Didn't pace. Didn't rage. He watched, listened, and took mental notes the way men do when they're planning something they don't intend on announcing.

Noah wasn't here to mourn his brother. Noah was here to finish what Jahi didn't get to. He sat at my kitchen island that first night back, elbows braced and hands folded. His eyes scanning the room like he thought the walls themselves might confess. Standing near the window with his arms crossed, Reid pretended he wasn't clocking every shift in Noah's posture, but he was. He clocked everything. The vibe between them wasn't hostile, but it wasn't relaxed either. They were two men recognizing the same threat from different points of view.

"Nuri, if my brother was killed, who do you think did it? I mean, you hired Reid, right? He's a private investigator and your security. Does he have any leads?"

"That's the thing, Noah. It could be so many people. Jahi had his hands in many cookie jars. Some he probably didn't tell you about, and honestly... that's the problem."

Noah nodded once. "He told me this was how it would be. He said if something happened to him, it would be crowded and confusing. That it would be loud enough to hide the truth."

Reid side-eyed me before asking, "What else did he tell you that you haven't told us?"

Noah's mouth began to twitch. Not quite a smile... more like him holding something back.

"He told me if he died suddenly, I wasn't to believe the headline. Or the police report. Or the convenient explanation."

"Yeah, he left me something telling me not to trust anyone either," I said. "That makes me sad. I guess he really felt his days coming to an end. He tried warning those close to him."

"He said someone would rush the story," Noah continued. "Push an angle. He said it would either be an accident, robbery gone wrong, or the wrong place at the wrong time. He told me that's when I was supposed to start paying attention."

I wrapped my arms around myself. "Paying attention to what?"

"To who got quiet. And who got comfortable."

That was when I understood the difference between Noah and Jahi.

Jahi loved the illusion of control. He loved the image. The rooms where power wore tailored suits and spoke in coded compliments.

Noah didn't care about any of that shit. He didn't care about being seen at all. He cared about patterns. Noah watched my phone when it rang. The news when Jahi's name was mentioned. The way certain people remembered to check on me after days of silence.

Reid didn't interfere. He adjusted. He tightened the perimeter around my life without making it feel like a cage. He trusted Noah just enough to let him breathe, but not enough to look away.

Once I was back in Atlanta, the girls called to set up a game night. Maya was out of the hospital and was doing well. I searched for a way to tell them about Noah, but instead, I would let them see for themselves and see how they would react. Reid thought it was a bad idea, but I knew it would make for excellent conversation, so I set it up to take place after I'd run it by Noah. He was all in. I also called Jahi's parents and told them I needed them to get here ASAP. That Jahi had some things he'd like me to go over with them in person. I sent them two first-class tickets for the first flight out. They messaged and told me they'd be here by week's end. Until they arrived, I'd have fun with the girls.

Reid offered to cater our little gathering. Noah had also picked up cooking in Barbados, so they made it a team effort. Wednesday night was upon us, and everything was set in place. Noah had gone upstairs to get dressed for the surprise. I told him to pick out anything he wanted in Jahi's closet, get dressed, and meet us back downstairs in about an hour. That would give the girls and me time to have a few drinks and loosen up. And one by one, they filed in.

Charity came first, carrying three bottles of wine. She looked like she'd already drunk two of them. Next, Paige arrived. Already talking, already loud, and already asking why Reid was standing in the corner looking like a sexy federal building. Maya arrived last with a casserole and a prayer, which felt aggressively on brand.

We ate, drank, and talked shit as usual. By the second bottle, Paige had kicked her heels off and was explaining... loudly... why spades was a Black spiritual experience and not just a card game, while Charity accused her of cheating with that "raggedy-ass face you make when you're lying," and Maya kept whispering, "Lord, forgive us," every time someone said a curse word.

Reid stayed in the background, arms crossed, pretending he wasn't listening while listening to everything, of course. The man had the posture of someone who could hear a rat piss on cotton.

We were relaxed, and their guards were completely down. In fact, they were too relaxed, and it was time to change the temperature in the room. Not dramatically or with a bang. To just shift it a little.

And then—behind us—we heard footsteps. Slow and expensive sounding. I turned toward the staircase just as he stepped into the light. There was Noah, dressed in one of Jahi's tailored suits. Perfectly fitted, dark, crisp, and familiar enough to make my stomach drop, and strange enough to make my brain glitch. For half a second, my heart forgot what year it was. For half a second, my body betrayed me. And then—all hell broke loose.

Maya screamed like someone had just summoned a demon in the living room. Paige didn't scream. Instead, Paige stood up, reached into her purse, and pulled a gun like she'd been waiting for this exact moment her entire life. Charity fainted. Just—gone. Out cold. Face-first onto the couch like her soul clocked out early.

"What the FUCK," Paige shouted, gun aimed, eyes wild. "NURI, WHY IS YOUR DEAD HUSBAND WALKING AROUND THIS HOUSE LIKE HE PAY RENT?"

"No," Maya cried, clutching her chest. "That's not of God. That is NOT of God."

Reid moved so fast I barely registered it... His hands were up, voice calm, and he had positioned himself between Paige's weapon and Noah's face.

"Everybody relax," he said. "No one shoot the twin."

"The WHAT?" Paige yelled.

"I am not a ghost," Noah said calmly, hands raised. "And I would very much appreciate it if the woman with the Glock stopped pointing it at my face."

That did not help.

"YOU SOUND LIKE HIM TOO," Paige screamed. "I HATE THIS PLACE."

"Nuri..." Maya whimpered. "Baby, blink twice if we need to rebuke something."

I finally found my voice. "PAIGE. PUT. THE. GUN. DOWN."

She didn't move. "He got on your husband's suit," she said accusingly. "That's serial killer behavior."

"It was in the closet," Noah said. "It fit."

"That's WORSE."

Charity groaned from the couch. "If this is hell, I want my wine and cheese. I don't care if it's melted."

Eventually... through threats, reassurance, and Maya praying out loud like she was negotiating with heaven, I calmed them down. Paige holstered her gun but kept staring like she might change her mind.

Noah sat. And then quietly and plainly... he told his story.

He talked about the streets of Chicago. His addiction and his struggle, and the twin he didn't know existed until a DNA test told the truth. He talked about Jahi finding him, giving him grace, and saving him from himself. He called him an angel with the same face. He swore he was the bad side of Jahi but told us, the more he learned about his brother, the more he realized how much they were alike.

By the time he finished, the room was silent. Even Paige.

She tilted her head, eyes narrowed, lips pursed. "So let me get this straight."

Noah nodded patiently.

"You look exactly like my best friend's dead husband."

"Yes."

"You wear his clothes."

"Yes."

"You got the same face, same voice, same damn jawline."

"...Yes."

She sighed. Deep.

"Well that's unfortunate," she said. "Because you fine as hell. And I feel like I'm going to hell for thinking it."

Maya gasped. "PAIGE."

"What?" Paige shrugged. "I'm just saying. God knew what he was doing giving them both that face."

Charity sat up suddenly. "Wait... so it's TWO of him?"

"Yes... well, it was," Noah said somberly.

She looked at me. "Nuri, that man stressed you out so bad he multiplied."

I covered my face, and Reid cleared his throat, trying and failing not to smile. After all was said and done... we laughed. Really laughed, ugly laughed with our tongues hanging. The kind that heals but makes your mascara run and your side hurt.

With these ladies, Noah, and Reid inside... the house felt alive again. It felt dangerous and somehow safe. There were two versions of my past sitting in the same room. However, only one was breathing.

After the dust settled and everyone but Reid and Noah were gone, Reid and I went out on the terrace to have a conversation.

"Well, that was fun," I muttered, cracking a smile at Reid.

"Not at first. I thought Paige's crazy ass was going to blow Noah's damn face off. If not for blowing mine off first. Girl, you could have got all of us killed."

I laughed. "Yeah, I started regretting the decision the second he walked down those steps. He looked so much like Jahi. It was scary."

"Why, did those feelings start rushing back in or something?" Reid searched my face for the truth.

"Actually, no. Not at all. Well... I mean, my brain did glitch a little. Kind of confused for a split second, but I got back right," I chuckled.

"Are we going to talk about what happened between us the other night? We haven't discussed it since it happened."

"Reid, it's not like I'm avoiding it. We have 'company,' in case you haven't noticed. It's kind of hard to talk about fucking you when your dead husband is staring you in the face."

"Let me just say this, Nuri. The decision I made that night wasn't fueled by alcohol, delirium, or anything else. It was fueled purely by want. Actually, a need. I'd laid in bed that night... tossing and turning, and I couldn't stop thinking about you. About our interaction at the festival. About the way you look at me. About the feelings that were growing inside me from the very beginning. I got so flustered, I went to get water. That's when I heard you moan my name. I tried to ignore it and act as if it didn't send shivers down my spine, but I couldn't."

"Why not?"

"Because you are too special to me to ignore. I meant that when I said it to my mother, and now I'm saying it to you. I want more. More of you, more of this... whatever this is. But there is one thing I struggle with... I'm not sure if you truly like me or if I'm just a rebound. Someone told me a long time ago to never be the good man that came behind a bad man. Because if the woman isn't healed, she won't be able to tell the difference."

"First of all, I'm healed. Jahi and I had been over. We just refused to acknowledge it. Second, I call bullshit. I think it's exactly the opposite. Having a bad man for so long makes you appreciate a good man when he finally comes along. Whoever gave you that information needs to talk to an actual woman. Men can't accurately tell you how a woman feels. He can only assume."

"So, where do we go from here?" Reid asked.

"I don't know, but wherever we go, Reid, we go together."

Chapter Twenty-Six

Jahi's parents' flight was scheduled to land at 6 P.M. A perfect time to get them to the house, let them clean themselves up, and serve dinner. Talking briefly with Noah, I explained the love they carried for their son and how heartbroken they were when they learned of his passing. I told him I'd called her that morning I saw him the second time, and she had such a hard time receiving it. Maybe seeing him would mend something in her heart that was broken. Those were my thoughts and I hoped I was right.

I hadn't discussed it with anyone because I didn't need to, but I planned on giving his parents a few million to make living out their golden years a lot easier. This was the real reason I wanted to see them in person, but Noah's presence would serve as the icing on the cake. He wasn't

Jahi, but he was the next best thing. Maybe they could forge a friendship and keep in touch after being introduced. Since he had no family to call his own… maybe this could work. I hadn't planned to invite my parents. That decision had been made quietly and deliberately. I didn't want to open up a wound that was finally scabbing over.

But then my father called. His voice softer than usual.

"Your mother's been… dealing with a lot," he said carefully. "She knows things haven't been right between you two, and she feels terrible, Nuri. She wants to see you and make things right."

That phrase almost made me laugh in his face. "Dad, she's about thirty-seven years too late for that, but if you agree to come with her, it's fine. Please arrive around 8 P.M. I've got a special guest coming that I want you to meet."

Reid and I got started early. We lit candles. Pulled out the good china, real silver, and the same good glassware my mother used to reserve for donors, judges, and men she thought she could use one day. We set the table beautifully, and I even added a few centerpieces to up the elegance. The house smelled like money and good intentions. Everything was carefully planned. The menu… the decorations. Once they landed, I had Reid send a driver to retrieve them and bring them back to the house. I knew this reveal would shock everyone but bring comfort at the same time. Comfort to Jahi's parents and mine.

Jahi's parents arrived first. Mine followed soon after. My father kissed my cheek, and my mother smiled at me like we were strangers passing in public. I watched them all move through my house, through my life, through the space Jahi should have still been occupying. Suddenly, a feeling of dread washed over me, but I sucked it up and pressed forward. With Reid protecting from the back, we talked, ate, drank, then it was time.

I stood.

"I have someone I want you all to meet," I said calmly.

My mother smiled while Jahi's mother stiffened. I nodded once. The footsteps from upstairs echoed just enough to draw attention without spectacle. When Noah stepped into view, wearing Jahi's suit like it had been made for him… the room cracked open.

Time seemed to stall. Jahi's mother gasped. Before I could open my mouth to introduce Noah… the bottom fell out.

His father went pale. Dead pale. Like all the blood in his face had ducked and ran for cover. I tried once again to introduce Noah, but like a gift wrapped in madness, they cut me off and they started talking.

"No," Jahi's mother whispered. "It can't be." Her

hands flying to her chest. "We saw you. You were dead. You were—"

Jahi's father dropped his glass. It shattered across the table top."Jesus Christ—you're dead," he said hoarsely. "We saw you. This isn't fucking funny." He stood up and backed away like the devil himself had just walked into the room.

My mother's knees buckled.

My father turned slowly. "What is going on?"

Noah said nothing. He didn't have to. His silence was a mirror, and they couldn't stand what they saw reflected back at them.I didn't move. I didn't speak. I just watched. That's when I realized something terrifying and liberating all at once. They weren't shocked because he looked like Jahi. They were terrified because they thought Jahi wasn't really dead and I didn't tell them anything different. The truth began clawing it's way to the top right in front of Noah and I.

"It can't be him," Jahi's mother sobbed. "We watched them close the casket."

My mother's voice cut through, shrill, panicked, and cinematic as usual. "This is crazy. What kind of sick shit are you trying to pull, Nuri?"

That's when Jahi's father snapped.

"You said it was handled."

Silence.

"You said once he was gone... that everything was good," Jahi's mother cried, turning on my mother with desperation dripping from her tongue. "The questions. The audits. The transfers."

My father's face drained of color. "Transfers?"

My mother finally spoke, and when she did, the mask slipped completely.

"He was digging," she said. "Digging into Greystone like it was his right. Greystone was mine. I built it. I controlled it, and your husband"—she scoffed, pointing at me—"started asking questions. Following money. The offshore accounts. Accounts he was never supposed to see."

My chest tightened.

"He was going to expose us," she continued. Her voice now shaking. Unraveling. "He was going to fuck up everything. So when Jahi's parents came to us—angry, jealous, and bitter over money they thought they were entitled to... we realized our interests aligned."

I felt like I was going to throw up.

My father stared at her, devastated. "You stole from our company and set that boy up?"

"I protected it," she snapped. "From him."

Jahi's mother let out a bitter laugh through her tears. "Protected it? Please. You were terrified he'd expose you. We were just tired of being treated like charity cases."

Jahi's father nodded frantically. "We thought there'd be a payout. We thought we'd finally get what was owed to us."

"Owed?" I screamed, standing now. "You greedy, jealous pieces of shit."

She straightened, eyes wild. "He forgot where he came from. He forgot who raised him and sacrificed everything we had to make sure he was somebody. He bought us a house and a Cadillac and thought that was enough." She scoffed.

Her husband nodded. "We were entitled to more. He wouldn't even discuss it. Said he had plans. Investments. Like we were a fucking afterthought."

Noah's eyes bucked. He looked like he was going to explode.

My father staggered to his feet. "You did this behind my back?" he muttered, his voice shaking. "You planned this without me?"

My mother didn't even flinch. "You would have tried to stop me."

Jahi's mother interrupted. "Before you—Jahi told us we were beneficiaries. That he had a policy. After he married YOU, he took our names off and replaced it with yours. We were supposed to get paid!! When we called to check on it, we couldn't get any information. We were no longer on the paperwork."

My ears started to ring.

"Nuri," my mother yelled. "You should be thanking us for trying to take this arrogant son of a bitch off your hands," she muttered as she pointed at Noah. "You didn't want him anymore and he didn't want you or else he wouldn't have been fucking everything that moved. We did you a fucking favor."

"Favor," I yelled. You muthafuckas had my husband killed over money. All of you will rot in hell. Especially you, Mr. And Mrs. Laurent. He loved you and you traded his life for money that you will never get."

"What do you mean we traded his life?" His father said loudly. "The bastard is standing right there."

That's not Jahi. That is his twin brother, Noah.

Gasped rang out through the entire room as the sirens wailed outside.

Reid entered the room. "Police are here," he said. "And just so you know... every confession tonight? Recorded. Audio. Video. Multiple angles. Y'all's asses are going to jail."

Detective Dollars walked in like judgment himself.

Jahi's parents screamed when the cuffs went on. My mother didn't. She just looked at me as they took her away, like she still believed she'd won something. She hadn't won shit but a pair of shiny new bracelets and enough charges to lock her away for life.

I walked to Noah, stared into his eyes, and hugged him tight. As he embraced me, I felt like I couldn't breathe. They didn't get his money. They didn't get his legacy. And they sure as hell didn't get to rewrite his death. I took everything from them, and I'd live the rest of my life making sure they never forgot it.

THE GIRLS CAME over the next day, unannounced but right on time. They needed to inspect the damage with their own eyes. All three filed into the living room, staring at me as if I was some kind of exhibit.

Paige spoke first. "Damn, girl," she said slowly, dragging the word out as she turned in a slow circle. "I swear on my future unborn children... I wish we had been here last night when all that shit went down."

"I would've given anything to be a fly on the wall. No—scratch that. I would've been a chair. A lamp. A fucking waterbug. Anything," Charity muttered.

Maya shook her head, already pouring drinks and handing them out like this was a celebration. "Normally, I'd be against the drinking, but I think this occasion calls for it. Do you understand how SICK I am that I missed your mama confessing to murder in your living room? Now you know I don't curse, but that bitch and her cronies are responsible for this knot in my head that won't go down. Not to mention this stab wound in my body. Like, all this is crazy work and is not of the kingdom."

Paige leaned across the counter, lowering her voice like the walls might still be listening. "No, because tell me why I woke up mad at your mama. I don't even know her like that, and I've been fantasizing about dragging her by her wig since the news broke."

Charity snapped her fingers. "THANK YOU. I told my therapist this morning that I wanted to fight an elderly woman, and she tried to unpack it. Ain't shit to unpack. Sometimes violence is just the answer."

"Not violence," Maya corrected calmly. "Community service."

They all cackled.

"I'm just saying," Paige continued, pointing her glass at me, "if you had texted 'girls pull up, the parents are about to expose themselves as villains,' I would've been here with snacks and bail money."

"You don't even eat during stress," I reminded her.

"That's a lie," she said. "I eat other people's trauma and drama."

Charity leaned forward, eyes gleaming. "So let me get this straight. Your mama said 'yes, I plotted murder,' your in-laws said 'yes, we wanted the insurance money,' and your husband's twin just stood there like the ghost of Christmas consequences?"

I nodded. "Didn't say a word."

Paige threw her hands in the air. "MEN. Why is it always the quiet ones doing psychological warfare?"

Charity cackled. "The way I would've fake fainted just to see who tried to help me."

"You would've actually fainted," Maya said. "Out of excitement."

"Correct." She giggled.

"Speaking of the ghost of Christmas consequences... where is his fine ass at anyway?" Paige questioned.

"You know, I know he isn't my husband, but I still don't know how I feel about you crushing on my brother-in-law. He has my husband's entire face, for fuck's sake."

Paige shot back, "Does he have his dick too? Because you said before that the draws were banging. I'm asking for a friend."

We all cackled. They started talking over each other then, the room filling with overlapping commentary and outrage and jokes so wild I couldn't even keep up...Paige suggesting a reality show deal, Maya swearing she'd have flipped a table like Jesus, Charity insisting she would've locked the doors, and made everyone keep talking just to see how deep the mess went.

"And don't even get me started," Paige said, standing now, pacing, fully worked up, "on the fact that your mama tried to play remorseful once she was in the backseat of that damn paddy wagon. Like, ma'am....BITCH, you don't get to cry now. That window closed when you chose greed."

"Exactly," Charity added. "She had years to be a good mother and chose to be a criminal. That's a personal choice."

I watched them, my girls, my chaos, my lifeline and felt something that had nothing to do with justice or revenge.

They were angry for me. They were laughing with me. And most of all... they were here.

Maya looked at me then, softer, quieter. "You okay, though? Like... really?"

Nodding yes, I surprised myself with how true it felt. "Yeah. I am. I'm tired, but I'm okay."

Paige walked over and pulled me into a hug that smelled like tequila and expensive perfume. "Good. Because if you weren't, we'd be planning crimes."

"Still might," Charity muttered.

For once, the house didn't feel like the site of a tragedy or a crime scene or a headline. It felt like home. And that, more than anything, felt like I won.

I SPENT the next few days decompressing and processing. Sleeping when my body demanded it and staring at the ceiling when it didn't. I replayed moments I hadn't known were loaded until they exploded. My brain was on overload. Everything I'd known about just about everyone had been a lie. My father was heartbroken. How he managed to see the good in my mother all these years was still a mystery to me. Witnessing what he'd witnessed a couple nights ago pulled the veil from over his eyes. I kept a close watch on him and called him every day.

Reid returned home to his mother for a week to give me time to adjust to my new normal. I missed him... but he needed to care for the woman that meant the world to him, and I was okay with that. He told me he would be back shortly and to call him if he was needed.

Without him, the house felt... different... open, although Reid had the place locked up like Fort Knox. He still watched the cameras from his phone and checked in often to see how I was doing.

Outside the gates, the noise never stopped. The reporters camped out like vultures with microphones. Shouting my name, speculating, and rewriting my life in headlines that sounded like something straight from a true crime podcast.

Widow Exposes Parents.

Greed, Murder, and Millions.

The Woman at the Center of It All.

The people were turning my life into a damn ID Network show, and there was no escaping it. I had to sit through it and let it burn. This was Atlanta. Something scandalous was always happening. A week from now there would be a new scandal, and my little shit would be forgotten about. Hopefully. Until that time came and the swelling went down, I'd just chill. I'd survived worse than gossip.

Noah moved through those days with a quiet I hadn't expected. Grieving the brother he didn't fully get to know. The rage he'd arrived with softened into something steadier once the truth was no longer a question mark. He and I both finally had the answers we needed, and the doubt was no longer clawing at our spines. He was prepared to kill for his brother. He admitted it one night while sitting at my kitchen counter with a glass of untouched water between his hands.

"I don't say that proudly," he said. "I just say it honestly."

I believed him, and I was grateful... selfishly, deeply... that he didn't have to become that man.

When I told him I was giving him the money—the millions that would've gone to Jahi's parents had they not chosen greed and envy over love—he stared at me like I'd lost my mind.

"They don't deserve it," I said simply. "But you do."

I held him the way I imagined Jahi would've if things had been different. If the world hadn't split him in two and scattered the pieces in different states. I kissed his cheek, laughed when he joked about finally being able to buy furniture that didn't come from the side of the road, and cried when he promised to keep in touch.

"I'm going back to Barbados," he said, smiling wide. "I'm going to buy my own place and move out of yours before you start charging me rent."

I laughed through my tears. "Get out of my house," I told him. "But not out of my life. Don't disappear."

"I won't," he promised. "We are family now, and you can't get rid of me that easily."

After Noah left, the calls from Mercury started again, like a bad habit he couldn't quit.

I answered once. Just once, because I was not up for playing his damn games anymore.

"Whatever you're looking for," I told him calmly, "it's not with me. Take it up with your past lover."

He scoffed. "That bitch is going down, and whatever she owes me, you're going to pay."

"I wish the fuck I would. My mother ruined shit for you, not me. It was that bitch and her need to consume everything in her path. It was her greed and hers alone, so that's where your anger should be directed."

I hung up before he could respond. I didn't owe anyone access to me anymore... not my grief, my time, or my forgiveness.

The gates stayed closed. The reporters eventually left, and the house was exhaling again.

When Noah left, the house went quiet in a way that didn't feel lonely—just finished.

It was Reid who filled the silence. Not loudly and not all at once, but steadily. Reid and I both understood that love after trauma didn't need fireworks. It needed patience. We didn't announce anything, and we didn't rush. We just chose each other one day at a time until it became obvious that "exclusive" was just a word for what we were already doing.

Atlanta didn't greet me gently when I decided to step out. I wasn't expecting it to, nor did I give a damn. The city was watching, remembering, and whispering. But this time, I didn't lower my head or soften my steps to make myself easier to digest. I reintroduced myself the way you do when you've survived something that was meant to end you. I was unapologetic, head held high, and my hand resting comfortably on Reid's arm.

People stared... of course they did, but in my mind, what was understood didn't have to be explained. Besides, I wasn't explaining shit to anyone who hadn't bled with me. Reid didn't flinch... he never did. He stood beside me like he belonged there. Being his usual self... calm, grounded, watchful, and unbothered by the chatter. Atlanta didn't intimidate him. It never had, and walking into rooms with him felt less like being protected and more like being chosen.

We didn't rush love. We learned each other slowly, deliberately, with intention instead of urgency. We built trust the way you build a foundation... brick by brick, because neither of us wanted something fragile ever again. We wanted rock solid. We settled into a life that felt purposeful. It wasn't flashy, but it was rich in all the ways it mattered.

THE END

Epilogue

Peace didn't arrive all at once for me.

It came in pieces.

In the mornings when I woke without dread sitting heavy on my chest. In the evenings when silence no longer felt like a warning. In the moment I stopped waiting for the other shoe to drop just because history had trained me to expect it.

By the time Reid and I decided to jump the broom, my life had already softened around the edges. Not because it had become easy—but because I had learned how to hold it without letting it break me. We had learned how to hold *each other*.

Five years had passed.

Five years of healing, choosing, and learning how to love the right way.

With Reid, I never had to guess. He was steady, intentional, unmoved by chaos. He didn't love loudly—he loved **completely**. There was never a question of where I stood with him because that wasn't how he moved. Reid showed up. Every day. In every way.

We married quietly. Not because we were hiding, but because we didn't need an audience for something so certain. My girls were there, of course. Paige cried harder than anyone and still found a way to crack a joke during the vows. Charity watched me like she was memorizing the moment for a speech she'd never actually give. Maya held my hands afterward and whispered prayers into my ear, sealing the moment the way only she could.

Reid's mother was there too. She couldn't speak, but she didn't need to. Love hadn't left her body when language did. It lived in her eyes, in the squeeze of her fingers around his hand, in the quiet pride that filled the room as she watched her son choose a life that didn't require him to disappear.

ALS had taken many things from her—but not her joy.

Noah flew in from Barbados with his wife and their son—little Jahi. Watching him hold his child felt like witnessing something sacred. A full circle finally closing. He had found his footing, his peace, his future. And in some strange, beautiful way, so had I.

We talked often—about everything and nothing. About the past without letting it own us. About the future without trying to control it. Barbados became our shared retreat, a place where the air felt lighter and the memories didn't cut as deep. It reminded me that loss didn't mean erasure—it meant transformation.

Atlanta changed too.

Or maybe I did.

I moved through it differently now. With confidence instead of caution. I no longer flinched at whispers, headlines, or rooms that once felt dangerous to enter. My story had already been told. I survived it. And everyone knew it.

Reid's company flourished—not because he chased power, but because he understood that protection wasn't about force. It was about foresight. Inspired by that, I built something of my own. A company focused on awareness and defense for women. They came to me broken, unsure, afraid of their instincts—and left standing taller, stronger, certain.

That became my legacy.

Not the scandal.

Not the tragedy.

Not the man I lost—but the woman I became.

Mercury was eventually arrested and jailed along with the pathetic partnering parents. One day while looking in the safe for important papers, I came back across those flash drives. I decided to take a look and discovered more names and proof of criminal activity. Mercury's name was at the top of the list. I promptly turned them over to the authorities. That was the end of Mercury's scamming, racketeering and drug dealing career. Can someone say RICO act.

Eventually all the noise faded and judgment softened into background static. None of it mattered anymore.

Because at the end of the day, I came home to a man who chose me slowly and completely. To friends who survived the fire right alongside me. To a life built on truth instead of fear and to peace that didn't ask for permission.

And then there was this...the quiet miracle I never planned for but received anyway.

One night, curled into Reid's side with his hand resting over my stomach like it had always belonged there, I realized my body was no longer holding grief. It was holding life. His child. Our future. Proof that love didn't just return to me...it multiplied.

Reid didn't say much when I told him. He just pulled me closer, forehead to mine, eyes full in that way that always meant *forever*. In that moment, I understood that everything I'd lost had led me here.

Not to survival.

But to legacy.

And this time, nothing was taken from me.

About the Author

L.L. Momon is a passionate storyteller who crafts emotionally rich, character-driven novels that explore healing, love, and resilience. Born and raised in Tuskegee, Alabama, and now residing in Florida, Momon brings Southern warmth and depth to every story she writes.

A nail technician by trade and an intuitive introvert at heart, she draws inspiration from the complexities of real-life relationships and personal growth. As a wife and mother and lover girl, she deeply values the strength of family, and that love radiates through the pages of her work.

With 8 published novels to her name, including her latest, The Widow's Hour, L.L. Momon is known for delivering raw, honest stories centered on strong, imperfect Black characters navigating trauma, passion, and redemption.

When she's not writing, you'll find her creating beauty with her hands, enjoying quiet moments with her family, cooking up soul-soothing meals, or binge-watching her favorite TV shows. Through every story, L.L. Momon reminds readers that even the most broken hearts are capable of healing and that love, when nurtured, is a force worth believing in.

instagram.com/authoresslImomon
facebook.com/authorllmomon
tiktok.com/authoresslImomon
amazon.com/author/llmomon
goodreads.com/authorllmomon

Also by L L Momon

Whittling Wood

Whittling Wood 2

A Savage and Her Wicked Ways

A Savage and His Lying Tongue

To Love the Broken & Unhealed

Loyalty Bound Me, Love Freed Me

No Longer Yours

The Author's Website authoresslImomon.square.site

https://linktr.ee/authoresslImomon

www.ingramcontent.com/pod-product-compliance
Lightning Source LLC
Chambersburg PA
CBHW030651020726
47493CB00006B/1975
* 9 7 9 8 9 9 4 8 9 9 4 1 0 *